ME

The Rags-To-Riches Wife

Silhouette®

Desire

Published by Silhouette Books

America's Publisher of Contemporary Romance

Special thanks and acknowledgment are given to
Metsy Hingle for her contribution to the
SECRET LIVES OF SOCIETY WIVES miniseries.

SILHOUETTE BOOKS

ISBN 0-373-76725-0

THE RAGS-TO-RICHES WIFE

METSY HINGLE

is the award-winning, bestselling author of series and single-title romantic suspense novels. Known for creating powerful and passionate stories, Metsy's own life reads like the plot of a romance novel—from her early years in a New Orleans orphanage and foster care, to her long, happy marriage to her husband, Jim, and the rearing of their four children. She recently traded in her business suits and fast-paced life in the hotel and public-relations arena to pursue writing full-time. Metsy loves hearing from readers. For a free bookmark, write to Metsy at P.O. Box 3224, Covington, LA 70433 or visit her Web si www.metsyhingle.com.

For Melissa "MJ" Jeglinski
A very special lady, an even more special friend

Prologue

Coming tonight had been a mistake. She didn't belong here, Lily Miller told herself as she stood at the door of the ballroom and stared at the elegantly dressed men and women. From the looks of the crowd and the amount of diamonds on display, every member of Eastwick, Connecticut society had turned out for the black-and-white ball. And she certainly didn't belong with them.

She should leave now before she started crying and made a fool of herself. But she couldn't leave yet—not without telling Bunny Baldwin. After all, it had been Bunny who had insisted Lily attend the masquerade ball in the first place. Bunny had even gone to the trouble of providing her with a proper gown to wear to the fund-raising event.

Remembering the gown, Lily smoothed the skirt with her gloved fingertips. The strapless black confection with the tulle petticoat was the most beautiful thing she'd ever seen.

It was a dress for a princess. Only she wasn't a princess. She was no one—not even someone's daughter. Fighting back tears, Lily tried not to think of the detective's phone call an hour ago, informing her that he'd hit another dead end in the search for her mother.

Face it, Lily. If the woman had wanted you, she never would have left you in that church all those years ago. It's time to stop wasting time and money searching for someone who doesn't want you, who never wanted you.

"Dance with me."

Lily blinked, then found herself staring up into the blue eyes of a tall, dark-haired stranger. He was dressed in a tuxedo and wearing a black mask, and for a moment she wondered whether he was real or if she had imagined him. "Pardon?"

"Come dance with me," he said and extended his hand.

"Thank you, but I'm not—"

"How can you say no when they're playing our song?"

"Our song?" Lily repeated and recognized the first chords of "Music of the Night" from *Phantom of the Opera.* "How can we have a song when we don't even know one another?"

"Why don't we change that?" he said and, taking her hand, he led her to the dance floor.

Lily didn't resist. And the moment he took her into his arms, it was as though a magical web engulfed her. All the pain seemed to dissolve. All she could see were those unwavering blue eyes, looking at her as though she were the only person in the world. All she could feel was the warmth of his body pressed against hers, the heat of his breath on her neck. There was something exciting yet safe about the masks. With the mask, she wasn't unwanted, unloved Lily Miller. With the mask, she was a woman who was desired, a woman for whom there was no past, no future, only now.

One dance spun into another and another and another still.

And when he led her outdoors onto the terrace and kissed her, she didn't feel the chill in the air. All she felt was the strength of his arms, the hunger in his kiss.

"It's almost midnight. The ball will be over soon," he whispered.

"I know."

"I don't want the night to end."

"Neither do I," she admitted and he kissed her again. He tasted of champagne. He tasted of desire and every nerve in her body sang beneath the feel of his mouth.

"Then don't let it," he told her. Reaching into his pocket, he removed a hotel key card. "I'm staying in the hotel tonight. Room 503. Meet me."

Nervous, Lily reached for the gold locket at her throat, the disc bearing the initial *L*, that she'd been wearing when the nun had found her in the church. Only the locket wasn't there. She'd taken it off after the detective's call, she remembered. And for the first time in her life she didn't have her locket to hold on to, to remind her that she was reliable, sensible Lily Miller.

"Will you come?" he asked.

Taking the key card, she said, "Yes."

One

Her secret was safe, Lily Miller reminded herself again as she stared past the sea of mourners to the casket. A crack of thunder sounded overhead and clouds darkened the Eastwick skyline, causing the mid-May temperatures to dip below the fifty-degree mark.

"Ashes to ashes. Dust to dust," the minister began.

Tears welled in Lily's eyes and she reached into her coat pocket to retrieve a tissue. Dabbing at her eyes, she thought of the woman she had come to mourn—Lucinda "Bunny" Baldwin, the darling of Eastwick, Connecticut, society, the editor of the titillating *Eastwick Social Diary* and the woman who, oddly enough, had been her friend. How was it possible that she was dead, the victim of a heart attack at age fifty-two?

Lily thought back to the last time she had seen Bunny—only two days ago. She had been so vibrant, all excited about some juicy new tidbit of gossip that, no doubt, would have appeared in one of her upcoming issues of the *Diary*.

"We commend the soul of our sister, Lucinda, to You, Lord," the minister continued.

Guilt tugged at Lily as she remembered Bunny's knowing looks during the past few months. It had been because of those knowing looks that Lily had tried to avoid crossing paths with the other woman for weeks now. But two days ago her luck had run out. Bunny had arrived early for the Eastwick Cares board meeting and she had been unable to avoid her any longer. When Bunny had started to question her about the night of the black-and-white ball, she'd realized that Bunny had figured out the truth, that she knew her secret. Lily had even feared that it was *her* secret that Bunny planned to expose in the pages of the *Diary*. She had been prepared to beg Bunny not to say or print anything, only she'd never gotten the chance. The other board members of Eastwick Cares had begun to arrive and she'd been forced to leave or risk being seen by Jack Cartwright. Yet, as she'd hurried away, she had wished for some way to ensure Bunny's silence—at least until she could decide what to do.

Be careful what you wish for.

The old adage popped into Lily's head. She had gotten her wish. She had wanted Bunny's silence and now she had it. Her secret was safe. But at what cost? Overwhelmed by feelings of guilt, Lily squeezed her eyes shut for a moment.

"May she live on in Your presence, O Lord," the minister prayed.

Opening her eyes, Lily focused her attention once again on the minister and the service being conducted at the front of the gravesite. "In Your mercy and love, forgive whatever sins she may have committed…"

Lily shifted her gaze to the woman standing to the minister's right, quietly crying into her handkerchief. She recognized her immediately—Abby Talbot, Bunny's daughter. She noted the tall, intense-looking man with his arm around Abby and assumed it was Abby's husband, Luke. She had never met the man, but according to Bunny he traveled a great deal, something that had bothered Bunny. Lily studied Abby. Though she had met her only once, she had liked the other woman. In truth, she had been taken aback by the pretty blond socialite's warmth. She hadn't expected someone of Abby Talbot's social standing to be so welcoming to someone who lacked not only money and a pedigree, but any family whatsoever. Yet, Abby had treated her as an equal. A wave of compassion engulfed Lily as she witnessed the young woman's grief. She'd known from Bunny's comments that the two of them had been close. She couldn't even begin to imagine Abby's pain at losing her mother so suddenly.

Thinking of Abby's loss brought home her own. She had lost a friend. While she and Bunny might not have been bosom buddies, and while she had never understood the older woman's penchant for gossip, the two of them had been friends. And that friendship had been born out of their shared desire to help the underprivileged. Bunny had been fervent in her support of Eastwick Cares with both her time and her money.

But she hadn't limited her generosity to those who fell under the umbrella of the non-profit agency on whose board she served. No, Bunny had extended that generosity to Lily. She had treated her with kindness, and not just as an employee of Eastwick Cares. In many ways, she'd treated her almost like a daughter or, at the very least, a special friend. No one else had ever come closer to making Lily feel like a fairytale princess. Certainly not when she'd been a child shuffling in and out of the foster-care system. Then again, she hadn't exactly believed in fairy tales, Santa Claus or the tooth fairy. By the age of six, she had learned that life wasn't anything like the fairy tales. And while most of the families who took her in were kind, *she* wasn't a part of their family. *She* didn't belong. *She* never had. It was a lesson she'd learned quickly. As a result, she had never expected things like fancy clothes or party dresses. Those were for dreamers and silly young girls. She had never been either of those things.

But for some inexplicable reason Bunny Baldwin had been determined to have the grown-up Lily Miller experience the fantasy she'd never known as a girl—attending a party all dressed up in a beautiful gown and feeling as though she belonged. Bunny hadn't chosen just any party. She'd chosen Eastwick Cares' major fund-raiser—the black-and-white ball.

As if it had been only yesterday, Lily's thoughts drifted back to that day last December when Bunny had marched into her office and proclaimed that she had to attend the ball. All Lily's protests had fallen on deaf ears. Bunny had insisted that her employment as a counselor for the agency required she be there to assist at the event. That had obviously been one of Bunny's white lies—as Lily had discovered within ten minutes of her arrival at the ball. For some reason, Bunny Baldwin had cast herself in the role of fairy godmother to Lily's Cinderella. It was the only explanation for the society doyenne tricking her into attending the event and even presenting her with an elegant gown to wear. Oh, Bunny had claimed the dress was something that she'd found in the back of her closet. But she had recognized the quality of the beautiful black gown, Lily admitted, though it wasn't until she was in the powder room the evening of the ball that she had learned from one of the other women that the gown she was wearing was a vintage Dior.

Another bellow of thunder sounded overhead, jarring Lily from her memories. As the weather continued to deteriorate, Lily huddled in her coat and instinctively placed a hand on her stomach. She should leave now, she told herself. She had already taken a risk just by going to the church, she reasoned. Why push her luck? Every member of Eastwick society had turned out to pay their respects. And the Cartwright family certainly ranked among the city's elite. No doubt Jack Cartwright had been there among the hundreds of mourners who had filled the church. For all she knew, he was among the small throng who had gathered at the cemetery for the burial. So far, she had managed to avoid him. But what if he saw her? What if Jack recognized her as the mystery woman he had slept with the night of the ball?

Even now, more than five months after the masked ball, she couldn't believe her behavior had been so out of character. But then, she had hardly been herself that evening, Lily reminded herself. Just thinking about that day and how great her expectations had been when she'd awakened that morning sent another pang of disappointment through her.

She should have known better than to get her hopes up. If she had learned nothing else in her twenty-seven years it was never to expect something simply because she wanted it. Doing so had proven time and again to be a surefire path to disappointment. Yet, she had done just that. She had been so sure that this time it would be different. The detective she'd hired finally had a solid lead. She had believed that at long last she would have the answers she'd been searching for most of her life—who she was, where had she come from, why had she been left at the church all those years ago. Most importantly, she had believed she would finally know the identity of the woman whose soft voice and gentle hands were the only memories she had of her origins.

Only the lead hadn't panned out. She hadn't learned anything more about who she was or why she had been abandoned in the church with only a note saying her name was Lily and a gold locket around her neck. Lily reached for the locket that, once more, was on a chain around her neck. She closed her fingers around it and felt the familiar sting of disappointment. She had been more than disappointed that night. She had been devastated. Hitting another dead end when she'd believed she was so close had left her reeling.

She should never had gone to the ball that night—not in the emotional state she'd been in, Lily realized with the wisdom that comes with hindsight. But she hadn't wanted to disappoint Bunny after she had gone to the trouble of providing her with the gown. Nor had Lily wanted to jeopardize her job by failing to show up. So she had gone—only to discover she wasn't needed after all. Then, just when she had been about to leave, he was standing in front of her—the tall, dark-haired, blue-eyed stranger—asking her to dance. She had needed something, anything to block out the ache that consumed her. And once she was in his arms, all the pain, all the anguish of disappointment had faded.

There had been only him. The strength of his arms. The warmth of his smile. The feel of his mouth on hers. For one night, she had ceased to be sensible, dependable, predictable Lily Miller who had never done anything remotely reckless in her life. For one night, she had allowed herself to experience passion instead of just reading about it. For one night, she had followed her heart instead of her head. And because she had, she was pregnant and expecting Jack Cartwright's child.

"Grant her eternal rest, O Lord…"

Shaking off the memory, Lily took a breath, then released it. She scanned the faces of those gathered. Not surprisingly, many of them were familiar—members of Eastwick society, local dignitaries and politicians. Quite a few of them she'd met through her position at Eastwick Cares. Others she knew from the news or social columns. Then she saw him—the tall, dark-haired man standing two rows back from the minister. Her pulse quickened. Even without seeing his face, she knew from the set of his broad shoulders and the conservative cut of his hair that it was Jack Cartwright.

Of course, she hadn't known it was him at the ball. If she had known that the dashing man with the Tom Cruise smile behind the mask was the newest nominee to the Eastwick Cares board, she might have refused his request to dance. She certainly never would have accepted the key to his hotel room. But she *hadn't* known it was him. Or maybe she hadn't wanted to know. She'd wanted to believe that wearing masks and not exchanging names meant that she could steal those hours of happiness without consequences.

She had been wrong.

Yet, she didn't regret what had happened, Lily admitted. How could she when the result was that she was going to have a baby? Smoothing a hand over her stomach, she felt a flutter of excitement as she realized that in just under four months, she would be able to hold her baby in her arms. She wanted this child, had from the moment she'd discovered she was pregnant. After being alone all these years, she was finally going to have a family.

You are loved, my baby. You are wanted. You will always be loved. You will always belong.

Silently, she repeated the vows she had made to her unborn child the moment she had learned the baby was growing inside her. And as much as she already loved her child, she struggled once again with her decision to remain silent.

Was she doing the right thing by not telling Jack he was going to be a father? she wondered. But how was she supposed to tell one of Eastwick's wealthiest and most sought-after bachelors that the stranger he'd spent one night with was pregnant with his child? The answer eluded her—just as it had for nearly five months now.

Or was she simply avoiding the answer rather than risk rejection? She could handle rejection, Lily told herself. But her baby…her baby was another story. She didn't want her child, even at this stage in his or her life, to be unwanted.

As though sensing her gaze, Jack turned and looked in her direction. He scanned the crowd of mourners as though searching for someone and then his eyes met hers. For the space of a heartbeat, she couldn't move. She simply stared into those blue eyes. Suddenly his eyes darkened, narrowed, and she realized he had recognized her.

"May her soul and the souls of all the faithfully departed rest in peace…."

Lily didn't wait for the minister to finish, she simply turned and fled.

Jack Cartwright stared in disbelief. There she was—the mystery woman from the ball. He'd begun to think he'd dreamed that night, that there had been no beautiful redhead, that there had been no passionate hours spent in his hotel room, that there had been no woman with ghost-blue eyes and skin as soft as silk. But she hadn't been a dream. She was real. And she was getting away.

"Jack, where are you going?" his mother demanded in hushed tones as she clutched the sleeve of his jacket. "The reverend's not finished the service."

Beneath the net veil of Sandra Cartwright's hat, Jack noted the disapproval in his mother's eyes. It couldn't be helped, he told himself as he spied the redhead in the dark coat walking briskly toward the cemetery gates. "I'm sorry. I have to go. There's someone I have to see."

"But, Jack—"

Ignoring his mother's protest and the questioning look his father cast his way, Jack began to maneuver his way toward the rear of the crowd. "Excuse me. Sorry. Excuse me," he repeated in a low voice as he shouldered his way past friends, business associates and acquaintances.

"…and may perpetual light shine upon them."

Moments later, a chorus of "Amen" rang out and then the crowd began to surge forward while he continued in the opposite direction. "Sorry. Pardon me," he said as he bumped elbows and dodged hat brims. After he'd finally made his way to the edge of the moving throng, he rushed down a grassy slope toward the cemetery's entrance where she had exited. When he reached the wrought-iron gates at the entrance, he searched the street in both directions. But he was too late. She was gone, vanished—just as she had vanished from his bed that winter night while he had slept.

Dammit.

He jammed his fingers through his hair. She'd gotten away—again. And he still didn't even know her name, let alone how to find her.

"Jack? Jack Cartwright, is that you?"

Jack recognized the husky purr of Delia Forrester behind him. Gritting his teeth, he turned to face Frank Forrester's trophy wife. He didn't like the woman, hadn't liked her from the moment the seventy-year-old Frank had shown up at the Eastwick Country Club and introduced the statuesque blonde as his new bride. He considered himself broad-minded enough not to prejudge Delia because of the thirty-year age difference between her and Frank, Jack admitted. After all, he'd witnessed the success of Stuart and Vanessa Thorpe's May-December marriage during the last years of Stuart's life. Nor did he pay heed to the rumors about Delia spending Frank's money as though it was water. What he did hold against Delia was the fact that the woman had come on to him—and she'd done it practically under her husband's nose. He didn't trust Delia and, for the life of him, he didn't understand why Frank did. "Hello, Delia," he said and cast another glance down the street, hoping to catch a glimpse of his mystery woman again.

"I thought that was you I saw leaving the service in such a hurry." She looked down the street in the direction where his attention was focused. "Looking for someone?"

"I thought I saw someone I knew and I was hoping I'd be able to catch her."

"What's her name?" she asked and placed a hand on her hip, drawing attention to the way the shiny black all-weather coat had been cinched at the waist. He couldn't help wondering how the woman walked in the killer heels she had on. She tossed her platinum-blond hair back in a way he suspected was supposed to draw his interest, and stared at him out of brown eyes that were dry and clear, not a bit of smudged mascara in sight. She licked her lips, making the blood-red lipstick glisten. "Maybe I know her."

Jack considered that for a moment and couldn't help noting the marked contrasts between his mystery redhead and Delia. The chances of Delia knowing his mystery woman were slim to none. "I doubt it. She doesn't move in your circles."

"Well, I'm sure she'll be sorry to have missed you. I know I would."

Choosing to ignore the overture, Jack asked, "Where's Frank?"

She sighed. "He's waiting in the car. You know how weak he's been since his heart attack and since it looked like it might rain, I didn't think it would be a good idea for him to be out in this damp air."

"How considerate of you."

"I was trying to be," she said, a wounded look in her eyes.

Regretting his sharp tone, Jack told himself he wasn't being fair. Maybe he had misjudged the woman, he reasoned. After all, from all accounts Delia had seemed to pay considerable attention to Frank since his heart attack. "You were right to have Frank wait in the car. The damp air probably isn't good for him."

"That's what I told Frank. Unfortunately, being an invalid isn't easy for him. It's not easy for me either." She lowered her gaze a moment, then looked back up at him. "Frank's not the man he was before his heart attack. There's so many things that he can't do now."

"Then I guess he's lucky to have you to help him," Jack told her and decided he hadn't misjudged Delia after all.

"That's what Frank says, too. And I don't mind. Really, I don't. But every now and then it feels so overwhelming," she continued and took a step closer. "It makes me wish I had someone that *I* could lean on, someone who would take care of *my* needs for a change."

"Maybe you should get a nurse to help you with Frank," Jack suggested, ignoring the obvious invitation. He took a step back. "I'm sure Frank's doctor could recommend someone."

Temper flashed in Delia's eyes, but it was gone so quickly Jack wondered if he'd imagined it. "Oh, I couldn't possibly trust Frank's care to anyone else—not after that close call he had. Why, I don't know what I'd do if something happened and I lost my Frank."

"Somehow I think you'd manage. But hopefully you won't have to because Frank will be with us for a long, long time."

"Of course he will," she said. "But enough talk about Frank and my problems. What I want to know is if the rumors are true? Are you really planning to run for the state senate?"

Jack frowned. "Where did you hear that?"

"Never mind where I heard it. Is it true?"

He supposed it had been foolish of him to think that word

wouldn't get out, Jack told himself. He had been approached by a group of business leaders and asked to run for the soon-to-be-vacated seat. As yet, he hadn't made up his mind. He still wasn't sure he was ready to take on the demanding task of a campaign and life in the public eye—which was why he hadn't wanted the news to get out. "I haven't decided whether to run or not," he answered honestly. "But I am considering it."

Delia brought her hands together. "Oh, but you have to run, Jack. You'd make such a wonderful senator. Everyone thinks so," she said with a smile. "And of course you know you can count on my support."

"Thanks," he told her.

"You must let me host a party for you."

"I appreciate that, but, as I said, I haven't decided to run yet," he told her just as thunder boomed overhead. Grateful for the interruption, he noted the crowd beginning to disperse as the sky darkened and rain scented the air. "I should go pay my respects to Abby and Luke before the rain hits. Give my best to Frank."

Delia turned up the collar of her coat and glanced at the threatening skies. "You might want to wait until you get to Abby's." She paused. "You are going to Abby's house, aren't you?"

"For what?"

"The after-service reception. At a time like this, Abby needs the support of all of her friends. I'm bringing a layer cake."

"I see," he said, surprised. He wouldn't have pegged Delia as a friend of Abby's. After all, everyone in Eastwick knew that Abby was part of the Debs Club—the name the members of the country club had given the group of women who met regularly for lunch at the club. As far as he knew, Delia wasn't a part of that circle.

As though reading his thoughts, Delia said, "Just because I'm not part of the Debs Club doesn't mean I don't feel bad for Abby. I do. After all, I know what it's like to lose a parent. I lost both of mine when I was a teenager."

"I'm sorry," he said when he saw tears filling her eyes. "I didn't know."

"It's all right," she said and dabbed at her eyes with a lacy handkerchief. "I don't like to talk about it." She sniffed and shoved the handkerchief into the pocket of her coat. "I'd better go. Frank's waiting for me. But you should go to the Talbots. Maybe your lady friend will be there."

She wasn't there, Jack decided after spending the better part of an hour moving from room to room in Abby and Luke Talbot's home. She wasn't there, but practically everyone else was. Half the members of the Eastwick Country Club were there. So were most of the politicians, the newspaper editor and the entire board of Eastwick Cares. As he scanned the room in search of his mystery woman, he noted Luke Talbot excusing himself from a group and disappearing down the hall. He couldn't help but note the way Abby's eyes followed her husband.

A hand came down on his shoulder. "Jack, my boy, I've been looking for you."

Turning, Jack stared at his father. At sixty-eight, John was the picture of health. He kept his six-foot frame just under two hundred pounds. The tan he'd acquired from his weekly round of golf at the country club accented his silver hair and gray eyes. He suspected his father's recent retirement from the law firm accounted for his relaxed demeanor. "Hey, Dad."

"You looked like you were in a bit of a hurry when you left the funeral service. Everything okay?"

"Everything's fine."

His father eyed him skeptically. "You sure there's no problem at the office? Because if there is, you know I'll be happy to help out."

"Relax, Dad," Jack told him, knowing that his father had not found it easy to turn over the reins of the law firm he'd founded, even though he had wanted the freedom of retirement. "Everything at the office is fine. I just saw a friend at the service that I'd been trying to reach for a while."

His father arched his eyebrow. "Did you catch up with her?"

"I never said it was a woman. But no, I missed her." Not wanting to give his father the chance to question him further about who *she* was, he said, "You said you were looking for me. Did you need something?"

"Your mother wanted me to tell you that she brought a spinach quiche. It's one of her new recipes and she wants you to be sure to try it. It's in the dining room."

Jack grimaced. His mother was a lousy cook. When he'd been growing up, the lady had managed to burn, undercook and virtually ruin more meals than his stomach cared to remember. Unfortunately, she loved to cook and neither he nor his two sisters nor his father had ever had the heart to tell her how truly awful she was at it. Thankfully, their housekeeper Alice did most of the cooking. But his mother continued to astound them with new recipes. "Is it as bad as her liver mousse?"

"Nothing's as bad as her liver mousse," his father said dryly. "Come on, she's looking this way."

Jack followed his father into the dining room and was directed toward the quiche. Reluctantly he placed a serving on his plate. Looking up at his father, he asked, "Aren't you having any?"

His father smiled. "I had some last night. Now it's your turn."

"I hope my stomach will forgive me," Jack muttered and shoveled a bite of the quiche into his mouth. The egg-and-spinach mixture seem to expand inside his mouth and he forced himself to swallow it.

"Here," his father said and handed him a glass of water.

Jack washed it down, then shuddered. While his father chuckled, Jack took the remainder of the serving and dumped it in the trash. After wiping his mouth with a napkin, he told his father, "You're a better man than I am. I don't know how you do it."

"It's called love, son. Mark my words. Someday you're liable to find yourself eating something that tastes like dirt. But you'll do it with a smile because it makes the woman you love happy."

"Hopefully I'll marry someone who can cook."

His father shrugged. "Maybe you will. But then, I never married your mother for her cooking ability."

No, Jack thought. His parents had married for love. It was something that had always amazed him, how after forty years of marriage they were still in love with one another. He, on the other hand, had had numerous relationships in his thirty-three years and had even gotten engaged a few years ago until he and his bride-to-be had realized they were better off as friends than as husband and wife. But he had never come close to experiencing with anyone the kind of connection his parents shared.

Suddenly he recalled a slim redhead with ghost-blue eyes. He had felt something with her that night, something strong and powerful, something that went beyond the physical attraction and incredible sex. It was as though some invisible force had drawn him to her that night. And obviously, she'd felt it, too.

"Jack?"

"Sorry, Dad," he said, shaking off the memory. "What was that?"

"I said Tom Carlton asked me if you'd give any more thought to running for Petersen's seat in the senate when he retires."

"I'm considering it. But I just don't know if I'm right for the job."

"I don't see why you wouldn't be," his father told him. "You're a fine attorney, son. You're smart and savvy enough to work with those politicians and get things accomplished. Most importantly, you're honest and you care about people. Just look at what you've been able to do since you joined the board of Eastwick Cares. Everyone's raved about the program to battle illiteracy."

"It was a joint effort. There are a lot of good people on that board and working for Eastwick Cares."

"Bunny, God rest her soul, told your mother it was your idea."

It was true, but he and the other members had all contributed to making the program happen. "Even if it was, sitting on the board of a non-profit agency and sitting on Capitol Hill are two different things. I'm not sure I want to make that kind of commitment and jump into the political fish bowl."

"Well, you're going to have to decide soon. Petersen has just over a year left to serve before he retires and people are already lining up to toss their hat into the ring for his seat. Running a campaign is expensive and the sooner Carlton and his group know who their candidate is, the better."

"I told Carlton I'd give him my answer by the end of the month." And Jack knew he would have to make a decision soon.

His father slapped him on the back. "Whatever you decide, your mother and I are behind you."

"Thanks, Dad. I appreciate that."

His father nodded. "I better go find your mother."

"And I need to get back to the office."

"Make sure you call your mother and tell her something nice about that quiche."

"I will," Jack promised and as his father went in search of his mother, he headed for the door. In the foyer, he retrieved his gray raincoat from the closet and stepped outside onto the veranda.

The rain that had threatened earlier was now coming down steadily. Too bad his umbrella was sitting in the car, he thought, as he slipped on his raincoat. After turning up the collar, he slipped his hands into the pockets and his fingers brushed a piece of paper. Frowning, Jack pulled out a buff-colored sheet of paper that had been folded in half. He unfolded it and began to read the unsigned message typed in large bold letters:

WHAT WOULD THE GOOD CITIZENS OF EAST-WICK THINK IF THEY FOUND OUT THAT THEIR CANDIDATE FOR THE SENATE WAS ABOUT TO BECOME AN UNWED FATHER?

UNLESS YOU WANT EVERYONE TO KNOW YOUR DIRTY LITTLE SECRET, YOU'LL PLACE $50,000 IN SMALL BILLS IN A SHOPPING BAG AND LEAVE IT IN EASTWICK PARK UNDER THE BENCH ACROSS FROM THE FOUNTAIN BY NOON TOMORROW. IF YOU FAIL TO DELIVER THE MONEY OR NOTIFY THE AUTHORITIES, YOU CAN FORGET THE SENATE NOMINATION.

Two

Stunned, Jack didn't notice that the rain was coming down harder. He didn't notice that the pink-and-white blossoms from the mountain laurels lay scattered beneath the shrubs or that the branches of the white oak bowed beneath the weight of the downpour. He didn't even notice that on the other side of the door was a house filled with people. His entire focus was on the note he held in his hands. He reread it, and, as he did so, shock gave way to anger.

He was being blackmailed!

Or at least that's what the person who'd written the note had intended. Turning the sheet of paper over, he studied it, looked for something that might indicate who the author was. But he found nothing.

It didn't matter who had written it, he told himself as he crushed the note in his fist. Whoever had done so had made two very big mistakes. The first mistake was thinking that he would ever succumb to extortion and the second mistake was the allegation itself. The charge was flat-out ridiculous. He hadn't fathered any child and no one was expecting his baby. Aside from the fact that he wasn't involved with anyone, he hadn't even been with a woman since last year. Not since… Jack went still.

Not since the night of the black-and-white ball.

Suddenly, images flashed through his mind. Images of a moonlit room, of a woman with silken skin and ghost-blue eyes.

Was it possible? Could she be pregnant?

No. She couldn't be. They might not have known one another and, granted, the sex had been explosive, but at least they'd had the good sense to use protection. Then he remembered that last time they'd made love….

"You have the softest skin," Jack whispered as he lay in the bed beside her. He drew his finger down her back. She felt like satin—only warmer and with the faint scent of roses and something else. It was a scent he could easily get used to, wanted to get used to, he realized. But they had agreed at the outset that what happened between them tonight ended tonight. The masks they'd worn at the ball had made the evening both intriguing and exciting. They were strangers. Yet the physical attraction had been palpable. He still couldn't believe he'd given her his room key—or that she'd come. Her insistence that they not reveal their identities had seemed like a good idea at the time. There had been something dangerous and appealing about not knowing who the woman was behind the mask. Only now, he wasn't sure he should have agreed because the more time he spent with her, the more sure he was that he didn't want things between them to end. He pressed a kiss to her spine and when she shivered, he asked, "Ticklish?"

"No," she said, her voice a breathy whisper.

He slid his arm around her waist and drew her body closer, fitting her against him. No, he definitely didn't want tonight to be the end. Easing the sheet down, he kissed her bare shoulder and, when she trembled, desire stirred inside him again. It had only been an hour since he'd last made love to her. And already, he wanted her again. But this time, he wanted more than just her body. He wanted her. "I know we agreed not to exchange information, but maybe we should rethink that."

"No," she said, her body tensing.

"Why not?"

"Because it would mean going back to the real world. And I don't want to go back to that world. At least not tonight. Tonight I don't want to think of anything outside this room."

Moved by the desperation in her voice, he turned her over so that he could see her face. He trailed a finger along her cheek, saw something haunted in those blue eyes. "All right. Tonight there is no world outside this room," he told her. "But at least tell me your name. I can't keep calling you Red."

"I like you calling me Red," she told him. "No one's ever called me that before."

"But I—"

She sat up and pushed him back onto the bed. "Shh. No more talking," she told him and then she took the lead. She kissed him on the mouth, deeply, thoroughly. Then that hot, moist mouth of hers moved south. She kissed his neck, his chest, and moved lower. When she pressed her lips to his belly, his gut tightened. He reached for her.

Wondering what spell this siren had cast on him, Jack took her mouth, explored her body as she had explored his. Never in his life had he wanted a woman this way, a want that felt dangerously close to need. When he could stand it no longer, he reached over to the nightstand for the condom.

"No, let me," she said, her voice breathless. She ripped the foil package open with her teeth, sending desire slicing through him again. He lay back against the pillow and watched her as she slowly eased the condom over the length of him. The sensation was exquisite. So was the look of wonder on her face. He'd known she'd had little experience the first time they'd made love. There had been an innocence and an abandon in her response that had told him this night was something as out of the ordinary for her as it was for him. For a moment, he wondered why she had come to his room. What was it in that real world that she'd wanted to escape?

And then he couldn't think anymore because she was lowering herself onto him. Jack caught her hips, let her set the tempo. She moved back and forth, back and forth, increasing the pace with each movement.

"I...I can't," she gasped.

"Yes, you can," he urged, holding back his own pleasure, wanting to give her more. She gasped again and when the orgasm hit her, her muscles contracted around him. With each sound she made, each movement, he felt his own climax growing closer. When he could wait no longer, Jack flipped her over onto her back and buried himself in her once more.

And then the condom broke.

"Cartwright? Cartwright, are you all right?"

Jack reeled himself back to the present and found Luke Talbot standing in front of him, eyeing him skeptically. Shaking off the memory, he shoved the crumpled blackmail note into the pocket of his raincoat. "I thought I'd wait for this rain to slack up some before I made a run for it," he explained.

"I just came out to get some air," Talbot told him.

But given the look of annoyance on the other man's face, Jack wondered if that was the truth. He sized Talbot up, estimating him to measure an inch or so below his own six feet two inches. The man had what his football coach in college would have called a wiry build, but there was no mistaking that he kept himself fit. There was nothing remarkable about the brown hair and eyes, but the man always seemed to be watching. Just as he was watching him now. "I spoke with Abby earlier, but I didn't get to tell you how sorry I am about your mother-in-law."

"Thanks. It's been pretty rough on Abby."

"That's understandable, given the circumstances," Jack offered.

Talbot reached into his coat pocket and retrieved a cell phone which had obviously been placed on vibrate. He frowned as he looked at the number. "Excuse me, I need to take this call."

"No problem. I think I'll make a run for it," Jack told him and stepped off the veranda and into the rain to head to his car.

And as the rain slapped him in the face, Jack thought once again to that night last December. She'd been gone when he'd awakened the next morning. Despite making several inquiries, no one seemed to know who his mystery woman was. Obviously, the woman had known Bunny Baldwin. He closed his fist around the note in his pocket. Using the remote, he unlocked the door to his car and slid behind the wheel. After starting the engine, he wiped his hand down his face in an attempt to dry it. Then he slicked back his wet hair and stared out at the rain. She'd made it clear that she'd wanted no relationship beyond that night, he reminded himself. It was the reason he hadn't made a serious effort to find her.

Until now.

Sorry, Red. The rules of the game have just changed.

Lily dug through the files in her desk drawer. Finally she located the one for which she'd been searching and snatched it from the pile. As she shoved it into her briefcase, she glanced up at the clock and groaned. Twenty minutes past five. The board meeting for Eastwick Cares started in ten minutes and she didn't want to be anywhere near this office when it did. She should have been out of here long before now, she admitted. But when Kristen, one of the teens she'd been counseling, had shown up needing to talk, Lily hadn't been able to refuse. As a result, she'd cut it too close this time. The board members would be arriving any second.

Since seeing Jack Cartwright at Bunny's funeral three days ago, she'd been edgy. He had recognized her. Of that much she was sure. As a result, she hadn't been able to shake the feeling that the other shoe was about to fall. She locked the file drawer, then switched off her desk lamp. Grabbing her keys and purse with one hand and her briefcase with the other, Lily hurried toward the door. She had just pulled the door closed behind her when she heard the distinctive chime of the elevator. Six flights or not, the stairs would be safer, she reasoned and headed for the stairwell in the opposite direction.

"Miss Miller! Miss Miller, wait!"

Lily heard Kristen calling out to her, as well as the chatter of several people who had evidently exited the elevator with the girl. She wanted to ignore Kristen and leave. Otherwise, she'd run the risk of Jack seeing her. But how could she ignore a child who had come to her for help? She couldn't, she admitted. Stopping, she turned around.

"Geez, Miss Miller, didn't you hear me?" Kristen asked.

Lily walked back to the girl who had come halfway down the corridor to catch her. "I'm sorry. My mind was on something else. Did you need something?"

"I think I forgot my book bag in your office."

"Well, let's go see if we can find it," she said and headed back to her office where she unlocked the door and turned on the light.

"There it is," Kristen claimed, indicating the couch where she had sat during their session. The lime-green pack rested on the floor on the opposite side of the sofa. Kristen retrieved the backpack and slung the strap over one shoulder, then turned back to face her. "I've got an exam tomorrow that I need to study for and all my notes are in here," she said patting the bag. "I don't know what I would have done if you'd already left."

"Then I'm glad you caught me in time," Lily replied as she left the office with the teenager.

The elevator dinged its arrival again. "There's the elevator. You going down?"

"Not yet," Lily said, still hoping she could escape without seeing Jack.

"See you next week then," the petite brunette told her and rushed toward the elevator's opening doors. The elevator began to empty and Kristen stepped inside. "Thanks," she murmured to someone still inside the elevator, holding the door open for her. "Bye, Miss Miller. And thanks again."

"Good bye," Lily called out, and when he exited the elevator she could have sworn she heard it—the other shoe dropping. Because, just as she had feared for months, the man standing outside the elevator staring at her was Jack Cartwright. Unable to move, she simply stood and watched the shock in his blue eyes turn to fury as they moved from her face to her belly and back again.

He walked toward her. His voice was low and dangerous as he said, "Hello, Red." He paused then glanced at the nameplate on her office door. "Or should I say, 'Hello, Lily Miller'?"

She nodded, not sure she could even speak when her heart felt as though it were in her throat.

"When is the baby due?" he asked, his expression grim.

"In four months. But—"

"Which means that I'm the father," he said. "And if you're having any thoughts about saying the baby's not mine, you can save yourself the trouble because I'll demand a paternity test and we both know what the results will show."

"I wasn't going to lie," she told him and placed a protective hand on her stomach. "I just wanted you to know that getting pregnant…it…it wasn't something I'd planned."

"Neither was the condom breaking," he responded. "Why did you tell me you were on the pill?"

"I didn't. I told you that I was safe because I thought it was a safe time. You just assumed I meant I was on the pill," she explained and felt the color rush to her cheeks. "It's no one's fault. It was an accident, Jack—"

His head snapped up and he pinned her with his eyes. "So you *do* know who I am."

"Yes. But not at first. Not until later that night in the hotel room when you took off your mask," she admitted.

"You knew even then? And yet you didn't want me to know who you were. Why is that, Lily? Why keep up the pretense? Was it all some kind of joke for you?"

"No! No, it wasn't a joke," she told him, not wanting him to believe she had used him. "That night…that night I wasn't myself. I didn't *want* to be me. So when you asked me to dance and we decided to follow the rules of the masquerade ball and not reveal our identities, I didn't have to be me. It seemed…it seemed so harmless," she offered because she didn't know how to tell him that she'd been lost and hurting that night and he had made her feel whole again. "Going to your room that night…it's…it's not something I would normally do."

"Asking a strange woman to my hotel room isn't exactly the norm for me, either," he told her, his voice sharp. "So why not be honest? Why not tell me who you were? Why keep pretending?"

"Because I was afraid if I told you who I was, you would stop. And I didn't want you to stop," she told him honestly.

Something flared in his eyes. But whatever he'd planned to say never made it past his lips because a door down the hall opened.

"Cartwright, the meeting's about to start," Doug Walters, one of the other board members, called out.

"Go ahead and start without me," he said, never taking his eyes off her.

"We're taking nominations for Bunny's seat," Walters answered.

"Go to your meeting," she told him before he could respond.

"We need to talk."

"I know." While one part of her was relieved that he finally knew the truth, another part of her was nervous about what he might do. His family status wasn't lost on her. While being an unwed mother might cause a ripple or two for her, the news that Jack was the baby's father was sure to be a scandal for the venerable, respected Cartwright family.

"Cartwright?" Walters called out again.

"Go ahead. I'll be here when you're done and we'll talk."

He hesitated a moment, then said, "All right. But if you're thinking about running away like you did at the cemetery the other day, just remember I know who you are now. And there's not a place on this earth where you can hide that I won't find you."

And as she watched Jack walk away, Lily knew he meant every word. Even if she had someplace or someone to run to, she had no doubt that he would find her. But she had no one—only her baby—so she turned and reentered her office to wait for him.

* * *

"What do you think about Abby Talbot taking her mother's place on the board?" Jacqueline Kent suggested.

"She's not even thirty. That's kind of young to be sitting on this board," Doug Walters pointed out.

"True. But she's bright and personable and she's been very supportive of Eastwick Cares. Besides, it might be nice to have some young blood on this board," Mrs. Kent responded. "Look what a great addition Jack has been."

The discussion continued around him, but Jack's thoughts remained on Lily. He'd heard her praises sung from the moment he'd joined the board. The incomparable, efficient Ms. Lily Miller was adored by the teens she counseled and her reports were always neatly typed, complete and available for the board meetings, even though the lady herself never was. Now he knew why. She'd been avoiding him. Not only avoiding him, but keeping from him the fact that he was going to be a father.

A father.

He was still having difficulty wrapping his head around that idea, he admitted. But he didn't question for a moment that the child was his. He knew that it was. As she'd told him, spending the night with a stranger hadn't been a normal thing for her—just as it hadn't been normal for him.

"What do you think, Jack?" Doug Walters asked.

"Sorry, Doug. What was that?"

"What do you think about Abby Talbot taking Bunny's place on the board?"

"I think it sounds like a good idea. From what I understand, she's a smart businesswoman. She's been supportive of East-wick Cares and I think it would be a nice way to honor her mother for her years of service to the agency."

"All right, then. Why don't we take a vote?" Walters said.

By the time the votes were cast and the remainder of the

agenda covered, nearly two hours had passed. When Jack exited the board room and headed down the hall to Lily's office, he half expected to find her gone.

But there she was, seated on the couch with her eyes closed and her head resting against the back cushion. She was asleep, he realized. And since she obviously hadn't heard him enter, he took the time to study her. Until now, he had only his memory of her—the way she'd looked when he'd first seen her at the ball, a vision wrapped in black satin. The way she'd looked in his room with the firelight reflecting off her hair. The way she'd looked in his bed with her back arched, her skin flushed and her body tangled with his. So many times during the past few months, he told himself that he'd been wrong. She couldn't possibly be as beautiful as he re-membered.

He'd been wrong. She was even more beautiful now. Dark red hair fell in soft waves to frame her face. The face was a perfect oval, her features delicate, the mouth that had made love to him and cried out in pleasure was even more tempting than it had been all those months ago. Dark lashes covered the ghost-blue eyes that had haunted his dreams. The dusting of freckles across the bridge of her nose that saved her from being too perfect made her all the more beautiful to him. But it was the bulge in her stomach and the knowledge that she carried his child that made his chest tighten.

She opened her eyes and stared up at him. Within moments, the lazy slumber dissipated and the wariness was back. She straightened. "I'm sorry. I must have dozed off. I seem to be doing a lot of that lately," she said.

She did look tired, he realized, and there were faint shad-ows under her eyes. Suddenly concerned about her and the baby, he began spitting out questions. "Have you told the doctor? What does he say? Is it normal?"

"Yes, I've told the doctor. And *she* says it's perfectly normal."

Realizing that he sounded like some panicked idiot instead of a grown man, Jack sat down in the wingback chair across from her. He released a breath and looked over into her worried eyes. "Sorry about that. This has all been a surprise for me."

"I understand. I was the same way at first, panicking over everything. But I've had a while to get used to it."

"Too bad I can't say the same thing," he replied, angered anew that she'd kept the pregnancy a secret from him. "Why didn't you tell me about the baby? Didn't you think I had a right to know that I was going to be a father?"

"Of course you do. And I was going to tell you."

"When? When the baby was graduating from college?"

"I wanted to tell you," she insisted and he didn't miss the way she was plucking at the sleeve of the jacket she wore.

"Then why didn't you?"

"Because I didn't know how," she fired back.

"The simple truth would have worked just fine. All you had to do was say that the night we slept together resulted in a child."

"You're right, and I apologize," she said, her voice softer, her expression calmer. She tilted her chin up, straightened her shoulders. "I should have told you. And now that you do know, you should also know that I intend to keep the baby."

It had never crossed his mind that she wouldn't, Jack realized. He also realized that she could just as easily have placed the child up for adoption, and if she'd listed the father as unknown, he would never even have known he had a child.

"But just because I'm keeping the baby doesn't mean I expect anything from you. I don't. I made the decision on my own and I plan to accept full responsibility. So you don't have to worry that I'll make any demands."

"That was a nice little speech, Lily. Tell me, how long

have you been practicing it?" he asked and surprised himself that he managed to sound so calm when inside he was furious.

"I… A while," she finally said.

Leaning forward, he made sure his eyes were level with hers, and he said, "Whether or not you expect anything from me is irrelevant. I'm that baby's father and as its father, I not only intend to take financial responsibility for him or her, I also intend to be a part of the child's life."

"I see," was all she said.

It was apparent that he'd thrown her for a loop. But had she really expected him simply to walk away from his responsibility to the baby? To her?

"I'm sure we'll be able to work something out with visitation," she offered. "Lots of families do it. Of course, we'll have to wait until the baby's older. Then we can set up a schedule where we swap holidays and extra time in the summers."

"I don't think you understand what I'm saying, Lily. I intend to be a part of this child's life from day one—not four or five years down the line."

"But surely you realize a baby needs to be with its mother," she insisted and he could hear the thread of alarm in her voice.

"It needs its father, too. I have no intention of being a part-time father, one of those men who has visitation every other weekend and alternates holidays. I want to be a part of it all—the late-night feedings, the first steps. Everything."

Lily pushed to her feet. "I won't let you take my baby from me," she told him, her voice firm, defiance in her eyes. "I don't care who your family is or how much money you have, I'll fight you. I'll fight you with every breath in me before I let you take my baby."

"It's *our* baby, Lily. Our baby."

She folded her arms protectively over her abdomen. But her eyes never wavered as she spat out, "I mean it, Jack.

I'll fight you every step of the way. I won't let you take the baby from me."

Standing, he walked over to her. He had a good six inches on her and knew he could be intimidating. Hadn't he been told time and again that his strong physical presence was as big an asset in the courtroom as was his skill as a lawyer? But if she was intimidated, Lily didn't show it. She held her ground, stood with him toe-to-toe. With her claws drawn and her eyes sparking fire, she reminded him of a cornered mama cat, fighting to protect her kitten. And he couldn't help but admire her for it. "Do you really think I'm such a heartless monster? That I would take our baby from its mother?" he asked.

She eyed him warily. "But you said you wanted to be there for everything."

"And I do," he said and touched her cheek. "A baby needs a mother and a father."

"I don't understand. The baby can't be with both of us all the time."

"Sure it can. All we have to do is get married."

Three

"**Y**ou can't be serious," Lily told Jack, unable to believe the man had actually suggested that they marry.

"I've never been more serious about anything in my life."

"Then you're either crazy or you're a fool," she said and moved away from him. She retreated behind her desk, wanting the sense of normalcy and control that it represented.

"Why? Because I want to give our baby a real home with both of its parents? It sounds pretty reasonable to me."

"But we don't know anything about each other."

He walked over to the desk and took the seat directly across from her. "That's easily fixed. Ask away. What do you want to know about me?"

"Jack…"

"All right, I'll start. My full name is John Ryan Cartwright, IV, but I've been called Jack since I was in diapers. I'm single, never been married. My parents are Sandra and

John Cartwright. I have two sisters, Courtney and Elizabeth. My Cartwright ancestors were English Puritans from Massachusetts who were among the first settlers in the state. On my mother's side my claim to fame is Nathan Hale as an ancestor," he said.

"Jack, this isn't necessary," she informed him, because just listening to him drove home how truly unsuitable they were. She didn't belong in his world, never would.

"It *is* necessary because we've created a child together, a child who's going to need both of its parents. If the only way to achieve that is by the two of us learning about each other, then I want you to know everything there is to know about me."

Seeing the determined look on his face, Lily didn't waste her breath trying to reason with him. Once he was finished, she would try to make him see that marriage was not a viable option.

"Now let's see, where was I? You already know that I'm a lawyer with the firm of Cartwright and Associates which was founded by my great-great-great grandfather. I became the firm's managing partner last year when my father retired. I serve on the board of Eastwick Cares. I also serve on the boards of two other nonprofit agencies because I believe one person can make a difference and that by giving back to the community we make that difference. I own my home and have a boat that I like to take out on Long Island Sound whenever I get the chance. I gross roughly $250,000 a year from my law practice and have a stock portfolio that produces another six figures. My favorite food is spaghetti. My favorite dessert is bananas Foster." Rising, he came around the desk to where she stood. He brushed his knuckles along her cheek. "And I have a real weakness for redheads with skin like silk."

Lily closed her eyes a moment and, just as she had done that night in December, felt herself grow weak at his touch.

"Marry me, Lily. Make a home with me for our baby."

He made it sound so simple. Get married, raise their baby together.

"It *is* that simple," he told her.

Only then did Lily realize she'd spoken aloud. Needing to break the hypnotic pull he seemed to have on her, she stepped back and crossed her arms. "You're wrong. It isn't simple," she insisted. And she couldn't afford to make the mistake of believing it was. She'd done that far too often growing up. She wouldn't do it now. Not when she had her baby's happiness at stake.

"Why not?"

"Because we come from entirely different worlds."

"If you're talking about the money—"

"I'm not," she said. "But it is a factor. For starters, I don't own my home. I live in a rental apartment. My annual salary is substantially less than yours. I have a modest savings account and a small IRA account, but no stock portfolio. I have a five-year-old car and a bike, but no boat."

"Those are material things. They're not important."

"It's not just the monetary differences, Jack. You have ancestors you can trace back for generations. You have parents, sisters, a family. You know who you are, where you came from," she said, trying to explain. "Do you know how far back I can trace my ancestors? Twenty-seven years ago—to me. I do know that my name is Lily because that's what the note pinned on my blanket said and there's an L engraved on this locket that I was wearing," she said, lifting the gold locket. "As for the name Miller, it was the name of the street where the church I was left in was located."

"Lily, I'm sorry—"

"Don't be," she said and turned away, not wanting to see pity in his eyes, not wanting him to see the tears threatening in hers. "Surely you can see now that the idea of us marrying, even if it is for the baby's sake, is ridiculous."

"Why? Because you don't have some pedigree? Do you really think that I'm that shallow? That I would judge you on the basis of something as inconsequential as where you were born and who your parents were?"

"I'd hardly call not knowing who you are or where you came from inconsequential. For all we know, I could be the daughter of an ax murderer."

"Or the daughter of a king," he countered.

But kings didn't leave their babies. And wealthy, handsome men from prestigious families didn't marry orphans who not even their mothers had wanted.

She felt him come up behind her. "So maybe I don't know where you were born or who your family is, but you know what I do know?" He rested his hands upon her shoulders. "I know that you're kind and caring. I know that as a counselor, you've made a difference in the lives of dozens and dozens of kids. I know that because of you a lot of the kids who've come through that door have a chance to make it, because counseling them isn't just a job to you. You care about them."

Since she'd become pregnant, her emotions had been on a roller coaster. Tears which she'd seldom shed even at the darkest times in her life were now always just a look or a word away.

"I also know that while you may not have planned this baby, you already love it and that you'll do what's right for it." He turned her to face him, tipped her chin up with his fingertip. "And the right thing is for us to get married. To provide a real home and family for our baby."

"But we can do that without getting married," she insisted.

"How? By shuffling him or her from your apartment to my house? What kind of life is that for a child? What our baby needs is security, Lily—and I don't mean just financially. Our baby needs a real family and a real home with both parents there to tuck him in at night, to have both of us there when she wakes up from a bad dream. Don't you want our baby to have those things?"

"Of course I do," she told him. Being part of a real family had been the one thing she'd wanted all of her life. It had been what she'd put on her list for Santa. It had been what she'd wished for each time she'd blown out the candles on a birthday cake. And it had been the one thing she had never had. That she still didn't have.

"We can never give our baby those things as single parents."

She knew he was right. Yet a part of her couldn't help but feel disappointed. "What about love?" she asked and lowered her gaze. The one thing she had always believed was that when she did marry, it would be to someone she loved and who loved her in return. "Marriage is more than sharing a house with someone. What chance would a marriage between us have when we don't love one another?"

"Who says we need to love one another? We like and respect each other. We're going to share a child. And we already know that we're sexually compatible. There are a lot of very successful marriages that are based on a great deal less."

Lily jerked her eyes upward. She had been so focused on what a marriage between them would mean to their baby that she hadn't considered what it would mean to her, to him. "You mean you would want this to be a real marriage?"

He smiled at her and Lily felt that fluttering in her stomach just as she had that night at the ball when he had looked at her the first time. "I don't see why it shouldn't be. I intend to honor our vows and would expect you to do the same. Since I don't think either of us plans to lead a life of celibacy, it only makes sense that we would share a bed."

"I guess you're right," she said because everything he said made sense.

"I am. You'll see." He tucked a strand of hair behind her ear. "And I think the sooner we get married the better."

A wave of panic hit her. "But what about your family, your friends? What will they think? What will people say?"

"They'll think I'm a lucky guy," he assured her.

Or maybe they would think he'd lost his mind. Perhaps they both had because she was going to marry Jack Cartwright. She only hoped neither of them lived to regret it.

She was as skittish as a colt, Jack thought as he looked across the seat of his car to Lily. Her hands were clenched, her body stiff and she'd had him stop twice during the thirty-minute drive for bathroom breaks. She'd claimed it was a hazard of being pregnant, but he suspected a big part of it was nerves.

Not that he could blame her. He had surprised himself when he'd blurted out that they should get married. But within minutes of doing so, he'd realized it was the right thing to do. He'd known right away that Lily had way too much pride to allow him to take care of her and the baby financially. So he hadn't even bothered suggesting it. Besides he had meant what he said—a kid really did need both parents. And while he might not have planned on becoming a father in quite this way, now that it was happening, he wanted to be a real father in every way. That meant providing his child with the same love and security he'd known as a child. And the only way to do that was for him and Lily to become man and wife.

Once he'd made that decision, he had approached her objections as he did an opponent in the courtroom. One by one he had shot those objections down. He hadn't exactly played fair, he admitted. When she'd told him about her family—or lack thereof—he could only imagine how painful and lonely it must have been for her growing up. So he had used her own feelings about family against her and gotten her to agree to marry him. And before she could change her mind, he'd set things into motion—first by hustling her to the courthouse the next day to get a marriage license and now by taking her to meet his parents.

Jack thought about the ring in his pocket. She'd claimed she didn't need an engagement ring when he'd suggested they shop for one. He'd never seen her wear anything except the gold locket. And while it was possible she was one of those rare women who didn't covet jewelry, after checking into her background he suspected few people had thought to give Lily shiny baubles. He also doubted that she would consider jewelry as one of the basic necessities in life. He wanted her to have the ring. He'd even planned to give it to her when he'd arrived at her apartment to pick her up for the trip to his parents' home. But one look at her and he could see she was a bundle of nerves. So he'd decided to wait.

"Are you sure I'm dressed okay?" she asked.

"You look beautiful," he assured her. It was true. The silky skirt skimmed her still-trim hips and gave him a glimpse of those killer legs. The apricot-colored sweater top gently curved over her breasts and the large-grapefruit-sized bump in her belly. Were it not for that bulge, he would never have known she was pregnant.

"Is it much farther?" she asked.

"About ten minutes," he said. "Do you need me to stop again?"

"No. I can wait."

When he saw her plucking at her skirt, he reached over and caught her hand. "Try to relax. It's just brunch."

"I know."

But he knew the prospect of brunch with his parents and sisters had made her anxious. He assumed it was nerves that accounted for her allowing him to continue holding her hand for the remainder of the drive. "This is it," he said as he approached the gates to his parents' home. After he'd punched in the code, the gates swung open and he drove along the landscaped driveway leading to the house.

"It's beautiful. And big."

"Not big enough when you have two younger sisters," he said, hoping to ease the rush of nerves he detected. "All I can say is thank heavens for the mudroom. It's the one place I could go and not worry about being invaded by females."

She smiled. "I'm trying to picture you as a boy dodging your sisters."

"Trust me, it wasn't easy," he told her and pulled the car to a stop in the circular drive. Quickly, he got out and opened the passenger's door for Lily. He offered his hand, and once again she took it.

"Thanks," she said.

When the front door opened, he squeezed her fingers and whispered in her ear, "Whatever you do, don't eat anything my mother cooked."

Before she could respond, his mother was there. "Lily, I can't tell you how glad I am to meet you. I'm Sandra, Jack's mother."

"I'm pleased to meet you, Mrs. Cartwright," she began.

"It's Sandra, dear," his mother told her and ignoring Lily's proffered hand, she hugged her instead.

"Sandra, don't smother the girl," his father said as he appeared at the door. "I'm John Cartwright."

"Mr. Cartwright," Lily said and looked relieved when his father merely took her hand in both of his.

"Son," he said, acknowledging him with a nod. "You'd both better come inside before your sisters and Alice attack this poor girl on the doorstep."

"Yes, yes, come in," his mother told her. "I do hope you're hungry, Lily. Alice has whipped up a fabulous brunch for us and I made my famous liver mousse."

Jack leaned close and whispered to Lily, "Remember what I told you. Stay away from the liver mousse."

But Lily didn't stay away from the liver mousse. Jack bit back a wince as he watched her eat another spoonful, then reach for her water glass again. "Be sure to save room for dessert," Jack told her. "Alice makes the best strawberry short-cake in Connecticut."

"It's true," his sister Courtney chimed in. "She uses real whipped cream."

"It sounds delicious," Lily said.

"Jack tells us you're a counselor for Eastwick Cares," his mother said. "He says that you work with the troubled teens in the program."

"Yes, ma'am." She looked up, relief in her eyes as Alice whisked away the liver mousse. "Thank you."

"Lily's really amazing with those kids," Jack said. "The number of teens who stay in school and stick with the program has nearly doubled since she's been there."

"It's the kids who do the work," she informed him. "All I do is listen."

"Your family must be very proud of you," his mother responded.

"Lily doesn't have any family," Jack informed his mother and wanted to kick himself for not telling his mother to steer clear of the subject.

"What Jack means is that I'm an orphan. I never knew who my parents were."

"I'm so sorry, dear. I didn't know. Jack." She said his name sharply. "You should have said something to us. Now I've gone and embarrassed this dear girl."

"I'm not embarrassed, Mrs. Cartwright, and please don't feel you need to apologize or feel sorry for me. The truth is, I've always believed I was pretty lucky because I've never had to worry about living up to anyone's expectations but my own."

"She's right," Courtney said. "Is it too late for me to be an orphan?"

Everyone laughed and Jack was relieved to have some of the tension ebb.

"Well, once you and Jack are married, you'll be a Cartwright and we'll be your family," his mother said.

"Are you going to take the name *Cartwright* or keep your maiden name?" his sister Elizabeth asked.

"Actually, I haven't really thought about it," Lily replied.

"I think when I get married I'll keep my own name," Courtney declared.

"In my day, a woman took her husband's name," his mother said.

"Whatever Lily decides will be fine with me," Jack told them, wanting to end the discussion.

"So, Lily, have you and Jack decided on a date and place for the wedding yet?" Courtney asked.

"Not yet," Lily said. "Everything has happened kind of fast."

"I was thinking that next weekend would be good and unless Lily wants to have a church service, I thought we would just go to the justice of the peace." He looked across the table at her. "Does that sound all right to you?"

"The justice of the peace sounds fine."

"A justice of the peace? You can't be serious, Jack," his mother proclaimed. "A woman's wedding day is one of the most important days of her life. I'm sure Lily doesn't want to take her vows in some dark and dingy office. Do you, dear?"

"I really don't mind," Lily offered.

"It's hardly a dark and dingy office, mother. The building

underwent a million-dollar renovation just last year," Jack pointed out.

"That's beside the point. You and Lily deserve someplace more suitable."

"It's all right, Mrs. Cartwright—"

"It's Sandra, dear. You must call me Sandra."

"Sandra," Lily repeated. "The justice of the peace's office is fine with me. I really don't want a lot of fuss."

"Well, you deserve to be fussed over," his mother declared. "And I simply won't hear of you being married in any justice of the peace's office. Your wedding day should be a memorable affair for both of you and we intend to make it one. We just have to figure out where to have it."

"May and June are big months for weddings," Courtney pointed out. "I'm sure all the good places are already booked. My friend Sue had to reserve the Eastwick Hotel for her reception a year ago."

"Which is why we'll go to the justice of the peace's office," Jack insisted.

"Nonsense," his mother said and waved him off.

"Mother, why don't we just have it here?" Courtney suggested. "We could hold it in the gardens."

"That's a wonderful idea, Courtney. I don't know why I didn't think of it," his mother said. "Everything's in bloom right now and the temperatures are mild. The garden would be the perfect setting for a wedding."

"We can set up an arbor of roses and we should drape the guests' chairs with white covers and bows," Courtney suggested.

"Yes. Yes. And we'll have a white runner for Lily to walk down the aisle—" his mother added.

"Before you start picking out wedding china for them, maybe you should ask Lily and Jack if this is what they want," Elizabeth pointed out.

Jack mouthed the words *thank you*. He could have kissed his sister in that moment. At twenty-six, Elizabeth was seven years his junior. No one had been more surprised than him when the kid sister who'd gone off to college with her cheer-leader's pom-poms had returned home a serious young woman and enrolled in law school. It had also been a surprise when she'd chosen to work in the D.A.'s office instead of joining the family firm.

"Elizabeth's right," his father said.

"But, John—"

"Sandra, it's up to them," his father informed her. "Jack? Lily? How do you feel about having the wedding here?"

"It's Lily's call," Jack answered and looked across the ta-ble at her.

"Please, Lily," Courtney began from her seat beside Lily. She grabbed Lily's hand and Jack recognized the look Court-ney offered up to Lily. His baby sister had used that same sad-eyed look on him to get her way from the time she could walk. "Say you'll do the wedding here, Lily. Please."

"I hate to see everyone go to so much trouble," Lily told her.

"It won't be any trouble at all," Courtney said. "Will it, Mother?"

"None whatsoever."

"We can use Felicity Farnsworth. She's a wedding plan-ner," Courtney explained. "She's handling Emma Dearborn and Reed Kelly's wedding for them and I heard Emma say at the club last week that she turned over all the details for the wedding to Felicity and that she's doing a fabulous job."

"That's an excellent idea. I'll call Emma's mother and see if she can get Felicity today. We have a lot to do. I don't think we can afford to wait until tomorrow to get started." She looked over at Lily. "Lily, you'll need to tell me what flowers you like and—"

"Hang on a second, Mother," Jack said before things went any further. "I haven't heard Lily agree to any of this yet." He looked over at Lily. "What do you think? Are you okay about having the wedding here? Because if you're not, all you have to do is say so."

Lily looked around the table at the four pairs of eyes trained on her, then back to him. "I'm okay with it."

"Good, then I'll see if I can reach Mrs. Dearborn for Felicity's number. In the meantime, you and I will need to work on a guest list and a menu," his mother told Lily. "I'm thinking mini beef Wellingtons, a pasta station and maybe I could make some mini spinach quiches—"

"No," Jack said in unison with his father and both of his sisters. The joint protest did what none of them singularly could have done. It stopped his mother cold.

"But you all loved my spinach quiche. What about you, Lily? Do you like spinach quiche?"

"I...um...I'm not really a spinach fan," she said and dropped her gaze.

Jack smiled, proud of Lily and not at all surprised that she learned fast. "You heard Lily, mother. The bride doesn't like spinach quiche."

"Well, I could do a quiche Lorraine instead," his mother suggested.

"Darling, you're going to have far too much to do to bother with cooking," his father told her. "Why don't we let Alice and the caterers handle the food?"

She seemed to consider that a moment. "You're probably right. We do have a lot to do and not much time to do it. Courtney, would you see if you can get Mrs. Dearborn on the phone for me? And, Elizabeth, could you get me a notepad and a pen?" She stood and placed her napkin on the table. "Lily and Jack, let's go into the library and start making a list. John, would you tell Alice we'll have coffee and dessert there?"

"Of course."

The rest of them pushed their chairs away from the table and stood. Jack walked around the table to Lily. She had a glazed look in her eyes and he could only imagine how overwhelmed she must be. He reached for her hand and squeezed her fingers. "Everything's going to be fine."

"Sandra, why don't you ladies go ahead and get started?" John said. "I'd like to have a word with Jack."

Once his mother, Lily and his sisters had left the dining room, Jack waited for his father to return from the kitchen where he'd passed along the instructions to Alice. He hadn't been surprised that his father wanted to speak with him. He had hit his parents with the news about Lily's pregnancy and announced their plans to marry only the previous morning. Both of them had been shocked, but there had been no recriminations, no lectures—only their unconditional support and love. Yet he hadn't missed the concern in his father's eyes.

"Why don't we go outside so I can smoke a cigar," his father suggested when he returned to the dining room. "Your mother doesn't like me smelling up the place."

"Mother doesn't like you smoking those at all," Jack reminded him.

His father shrugged. "It's my only vice."

It was true, Jack thought. His father truly was a good man, an honest man who was devoted to his wife and family. It had been his father who had made him want to follow in his footsteps and study law. It had been his father who had taught him responsibility. And it was because of the lessons that John Cartwright had taught him that he'd known that marrying Lily was the right thing to do.

Once he'd lit his cigar, his father said, "Let's walk a bit."

Located on five acres, his parents' home looked like what it was—a wealthy family's estate. In addition to the five bedrooms and seven baths, the fourteen-thousand-square-foot house had every amenity: five fireplaces, a library, a billiard room, garden room and a gourmet kitchen. The place even boasted tennis courts, a pool and a pool house with a full kitchen, living room, bedroom and Japanese bath. Yet, his parents had managed to make the place a real home, welcoming and warm. He hoped Lily had found both his family and their home that way.

"Lily seems like a nice girl," his father said as he puffed on the cigar.

"She is," Jack told him. "She was pretty nervous about coming here today and meeting you. I think she expected you all to resent her for what's happening. So I appreciate how kind you've been under the circumstances."

"I don't see any reason why we should resent her. She didn't make this baby by herself."

"No, she didn't," Jack said. He had to give his parents credit. Since he'd dropped the bombshell yesterday about Lily's pregnancy and his intention to marry her, his parents had offered no recriminations or unsolicited advice. The only thing either of them had asked was whether he was sure the child was his. Once he had assured them it was, they had simply asked how they could help.

His father followed the path toward the small stream that ran along the property. Growing up, he had often walked this path with his father. It had been at the stream that his father had first told him the facts of life. It was here that his father had spoken to him about women and responsibility. It was at the stream that he had first told his father that he wanted to be a lawyer like him. Jack knew his father had wanted to come here for a reason. So he waited, knowing his father would tell him what was on his mind when he was ready.

"I had a call from Tom Carlton last night," he began. "He said he landed another major backer for the Cartwright for Senate Campaign. All he's waiting for is the word from you to announce your candidacy."

"Yes, I heard. He left me a message," Jack said, remembering the voice mails left at his office and his home. He had yet to call Carlton back.

"He was concerned because he hadn't heard back from you and wanted to know how to get in touch with you. I told him we were expecting you today and I'd have you call him."

"I'll give him a call when we get back to the house."

His father took another puff on his cigar. "You given any thought to how your marriage to Lily might affect your political plans?"

"I'm still not sure what my political plans are. But other than finding out Lily's feelings on the subject of me running for office, I don't see why my marriage has anything to do with it."

"It shouldn't," his father told him. "But Connecticut is a conservative state. And Tom Carlton and his group are right at the top of the conservative train. They pride themselves on their heritage and strong family values. They like their candidates and their candidates' families to fit the same bill. And as nice as I think Lily is, she might not be what they consider the proper wife for a senator. This unplanned pregnancy and quickie wedding might not sit well with them either."

Jack scowled. "Then that's their problem, not mine. Lily wasn't born with a silver spoon in her mouth. She's overcome enormous odds and made something of herself. So what you, Carlton or anyone else thinks of her suitability doesn't matter. I'm not embarrassed by her background. I'm proud of her for not allowing it to hold her back. And nothing you or anyone else says will make me feel otherwise."

"If it did, then you wouldn't be the man I thought you were," his father said.

"If you feel that way, then why the lecture?"

"Because I think you need to be prepared for people's reaction to your marriage to Lily. There are a lot of small-minded people, even in Eastwick, who will think she trapped you into this marriage and that you're ruining your political future."

"The only opinions that matter to me are my family's," Jack told him.

His father nodded and they continued to walk in silence. Yet his father's words reminded him of the blackmail note he'd found in his pocket a week ago. He'd dismissed it and would do so again, he admitted. But listening to his father's warnings now made him wonder who the author had been. He'd learned from Lily that it had been Bunny Baldwin who had given her the ticket to the ball. As the publisher of the *Eastwick Social Diary* and a maven for gossip, he wouldn't have put it past Bunny to have discovered that he was the father of Lily's baby. But the blackmail note had shown up *after* Bunny was dead, and unless Bunny's ghost had decided to shake him down for cash, it had to be someone else.

Maybe someone Bunny had told?

Jack frowned. The note had appeared while he was at Abby Talbot's home. Abby was Bunny's daughter and the pair had been close. It was conceivable that Bunny had told Abby. Despite the fact that Bunny had always spoken highly of this counselor named Lily Miller, the scandal would have been hard for Bunny to ignore. In fact, it was just the sort of dirt that filled the pages of the *Diary*.

He recalled how distraught Abby had been following her mother's death. Too distraught to execute a blackmail plan, he reasoned. Besides, Abby simply didn't strike him as a blackmailer. Her husband, Luke, was another matter. An image of Luke on the day of the funeral, slipping away and disappearing into another part of the house, coming outdoors to speak on his cell phone, came to mind. While the fellow was pleasant enough, there was something different about him—something that Jack couldn't quite put his finger on. The man had always struck him as a loner, but it went beyond that. Luke Talbot was...secretive. Maybe Abby had repeated what Bunny had told her to Luke in pillow talk. For that matter, Abby could easily have mentioned it to the Debs Club.

Jack thought about the five women given the nickname by the country club years ago. They were a close bunch and they had all been at the black-and-white ball. If Bunny had told Abby about him and Lily, Abby could have easily mentioned it to her friends at one of their luncheons. He thought about the other four women now—Emma Dearborn, Mary Duvall, Vanessa Thorpe and Felicity Farnsworth. All of them had been at Abby's house following the funeral. As he thought about the violet-eyed Emma Dearborn, he couldn't see her as a blackmailer. The woman had her own money. She had a successful art gallery and she was engaged to Reed Kelly. Where was the motive? As for Mary Duvall, the one-time wild child of the Duvall family had undergone a metamorphosis since her grandfather David's stroke. She'd become devoted to the older man—hardly the actions of a blackmailer.

That left Vanessa Thorpe and Felicity Farnsworth. Stuart's death had left his much younger wife, Vanessa, set for life. He could see no reason for the petite blonde to resort to blackmail. And as for Felicity Farnsworth... He had heard she'd had financial troubles following her divorce a number of years back. But from all accounts her wedding-planning business was doing great. If the lady was the blackmailer, she certainly didn't act like one.

"You think Lily knows what a hornet's nest your marriage and her pregnancy are going to stir up?"

"She's a smart woman. I'm sure she has an idea," Jack told him.

"You're probably right. But whispers and innuendos… they tend to be harder on a female. How do you think she'll handle it?"

"She's a strong woman. She won't let a little gossip bother her."

"I sure hope you're right, son. Because the way I see it, she's going to get the brunt of the talk and she's the one who's going to have to do most of the adjusting."

"Marriage is going to be an adjustment for both of us," Jack pointed out.

"True. But it's going to be her life that has to change the most. She's going to suddenly be a wife, a mother and have to take on the Cartwright mantle practically all at once. That's a tough assignment for any woman."

"I'm going to do everything I can to make the transition easier for her," he assured his father. "But like I said, Lily's a smart and strong woman. She's not going to let a few wagging tongues bother her."

"Take it from a man who's seen his wife through three pregnancies, it doesn't matter how smart or strong a woman is, when she's carrying a baby, you're dealing with a whole other woman."

"I'll remember that."

His father fell silent. He said nothing for a long time as they continued to walk. But Jack knew him well enough to know that he wasn't finished. Whatever else he had to say, he would do so in his own time.

John took another puff on the cigar and as they approached the stream, he asked, "I ever tell you about the first time I met your mother?"

"She said you met at a dance," Jack responded.

"It was at the military ball actually. I was a college senior and captain of my ROTC unit and she came with her cousin, Bess. I thought I was pretty hot stuff back then. And the truth is, I was. I had more than my share of dates and was in no hurry to settle down," he continued as they stopped on the bridge that spanned the stream. "Then I saw your mother. There she was standing in the doorway—this slip of a girl in a long white dress with hair the color of coffee and sparkling green eyes. I took one look at her and it hit me."

"What hit you?"

"The Italians call it the lightning bolt. And I guess that's as good a way to describe it as any. Because I felt this jolt to my system. I couldn't take my eyes off her. And I knew right then and there that she was the one for me, that she was the woman I was going to marry."

As he listened to his father, Jack couldn't help thinking about his own reaction to Lily the first time he'd seen her. There had been something about her that he hadn't been able to resist, too. And the truth was he hadn't been able to forget her either. Even with the shock of learning about the baby, the pull was still there.

"Unfortunately, your mother didn't feel quite the same way and it took me a while to convince her that I was the right man for her," his father added.

"How did you manage that?"

"I gave her some space and time to figure out for herself what she wanted. Once I took off the pressure, she realized what she wanted was me." He paused, looked at him. "I got the impression that Lily isn't quite as sure as you are about this marriage."

"She isn't," Jack admitted and the truth was that while he knew marrying was the right thing to do for the baby's sake, he had his own misgivings. "But unlike you, I can't give Lily the time to figure out that marriage to me is the right thing." Because if he gave her time, he wasn't at all sure she wouldn't change her mind.

Four

Maybe Jack had been right. They should have simply gone to the justice of the peace's office, Lily thought as she sat at the table in the Cartwrights' library. How did something that sounded so simple become so complicated? Once Sandra Cartwright had reached Felicity Farnsworth, the wedding planner had offered to come right over with books, pictures and everything needed to plan her wedding.

Her wedding.

Lily's stomach pitched. She still couldn't believe she'd agreed to marry Jack. In truth, she still found it hard to believe that he'd asked her. No, not asked, she reminded herself. He'd all but insisted.

He might have insisted, but you agreed, Lily girl.

It was true. She *had* agreed—for the baby's sake. She was doing it for the baby, she told herself, so that her child would have what she'd never had—parents, a family. Not just any family, she reminded herself. Her child would be a member of the Cartwrights.

They had not been what she'd expected, Lily admitted. When she'd first seen their home, she'd wanted to turn and run. She probably would have, too, had Jack not been there to stop her. Oh, she'd rubbed elbows with rich people before because of her job. She'd even visited a mansion or two for fund-raising. But she had never been a part of that world, never been welcomed into it with open arms—literally. She could still remember the shock of being hugged by the elegant Sandra Cartwright. She hadn't expected that. No, she had expected Jack's mother to be cool, to treat her as the unsuitable woman who was ruining her son's life. But Sandra hadn't. Nor had Jack's father or sisters. In fact, they'd all been so nice to her that she'd been on the verge of blubbering—another side effect of her pregnancy.

"We'll need to decide on what type of wedding cake you want," Felicity said, breaking into her thoughts. "Do you have anything special in mind, Lily?"

"No, not really," she told the voluptuous blonde who had breezed into the Cartwright home more than two hours ago with enough energy and enthusiasm to power a ship. Dressed all in black, Felicity Farnsworth had been as cheerful as the butterfly clips she wore in her hair.

"Not to worry," Felicity said and flashed a smile that lit up her green eyes. She pulled out another thick binder from her arsenal and plopped it on the table. "Let's see if we can find something in here that you like."

"Ooh, that one's lovely," Sandra said.

"So is this one," Courtney said enthusiastically. "And this one."

"That one looks like a Barbie-doll cake," Elizabeth said dryly.

Lily sat back and watched the exchange. There was something warm and endearing about the dynamics of the Cartwright family, the way they reacted to one another, the affection beneath the squabbles, the sense of belonging. They were a real family. She looked over at the twin fireplaces and the mantels filled with family photographs. More pictures fought for space on the desk and library shelves. Beyond the library, which spilled into the living room, she saw the baby grand piano, its gleaming top covered with more photos of Jack as a boy, at graduation, of Elizabeth at her sweet sixteen party, of his parents celebrating their anniversary, of the family gathered around the Christmas tree. Someday her baby's picture would be there. Her baby would be a part of this family. Her child would belong. It was the reason she was doing this, Lily reminded herself again. She just wished that she didn't have to mess up Jack's life to make it happen.

"This one is beautiful," Sandra Cartwright declared. "What do you think, Lily?"

Lily blinked at the sound of her name and realized all eyes were on her. She looked down at the book and there was the photograph of an elegant white wedding cake trimmed with sugar roses and real white tea roses. "I think Sandra's right. It's beautiful."

"So do you want to go with this one?" Felicity asked.

"Yes," Lily said and once again she was hit by the realization that she was getting married.

"Do you have any preference to the filling? Almond and butter cream are the most popular, but we can have the pastry chef do just about anything you like," Felicity informed her.

"What about one of those cakes where every layer is different?" Courtney suggested. "Tiffany Aldrich had one at her wedding. The cake had six tiers and each one was a different flavor. I had a slice of the Italian cream and it was to die for."

"Well, we can certainly do that if that's what Lily wants,"

Felicity announced. "Do you think you'd like the multi-flavored layers for your cake?"

"Six tiers sounds like a lot of cake," Lily remarked as she looked again at the photograph of the rose wedding cake, which consisted of only three layers and a small bride and groom on the top.

"That depends on how many people you plan to have at the wedding," Felicity explained. "Do you have an idea of the number of guests you expect?"

"I hadn't really thought about it. I just assumed it would be small, Jack and me and his family, maybe a few friends."

"But, Lily dear, surely you realize that Jack has a great many friends and associates, not to mention the friends of the family who would expect to be invited," Sandra said. "Why, I think at a minimum we'll have three hundred guests."

"Three hundred!" Lily repeated and she could feel her stomach drop at the thought of all those people watching her.

"There'll be no more than thirty," Jack announced.

Lily swung her gaze to the doorway where Jack stood. He was wearing charcoal-gray slacks and a white shirt, having ditched his jacket and opened his shirt collar. And she had never been so happy to see someone in her life, Lily thought. His eyes never left her face and as he walked toward her the knot in her stomach eased. He stood behind her, placed his hands on her shoulders. He gave her a gentle squeeze and Lily could breathe again.

"Thirty?" Sandra Cartwright said aghast. "You can't possibly be serious, Jack. Why, my garden club alone has thirty."

"Your garden club isn't going to be invited, Mother."

"But, Jack—"

"Save it, Mother. Lily and I want something small and intimate with just family and a few friends. If you can't do that, then we won't have the wedding here. We'll just go back to the original plan and get married in the justice of the peace's office."

"Lily dear, try to talk some sense into my thick-headed son," Sandra said. "Explain to him that it would be an insult not to invite our friends to celebrate your wedding."

"Actually, I'd rather we kept it small," she admitted.

"But—"

"You heard the girl, Sandra," John said as he joined them. "She and Jack don't want to turn their wedding into a circus. And I can't say I blame them. If they decide they want to have a big reception later, then we'll throw them one."

"Well, I can see that I'm outnumbered here," Sandra said. She turned to Felicity. "Evidently we'll need a cake to feed thirty."

Felicity jotted down details in her notebook. "All right. Now that we've taken care of the wedding cake, we'll need to decide on the groom's cake. Most grooms like a chocolate cake, but we can do just about anything. Do you have any preference?" she asked Jack.

"Chocolate's fine," Jack told her.

"Great. Now what about the menu?"

Lily could feel herself starting to fade. Yet every muscle in her body was tense as Jack continued to rest his hands upon her shoulders. Suddenly she flashed back to that night in his hotel room. She'd been both nervous and excited when she'd first arrived at his room. She couldn't remember how long she'd stood there waiting, debating whether or not to use the key. Sanity had returned for an instant and she'd turned around, prepared to go. Indecision had her still standing there when the door opened behind her. Jack had said nothing. He'd simply come up behind her and rested his hands on her bare shoulders. Then gently he'd turned her around, lowered his head and kissed her. And all thoughts of leaving had melted beneath the touch of his mouth.

"…we had talked about mini beef Wellingtons," Sandra Cartwright was saying.

"Lily, do you want the beef Wellington?" Felicity asked.

"I tell you what," Jack said before she could answer. "Mother, why don't you and Felicity work up a menu? I've got a busy day tomorrow and I'm guessing Lily does, too. I'm sure whatever you decide will be fine with us. Right, Lily?"

"Right," she said, grateful to him for arranging an escape.

He pulled the chair back for her, and Lily stood. "Just remember, no quiche, Mother. Lily and I are going to need you to help us with everything else."

"All right," Sandra said. "I'll make the quiche Lorraine for you after the wedding," she told her.

"Thanks," Lily said. "I'll look forward to it."

Ten minutes later, after saying her good-byes and agreeing to speak with Felicity the next day, Lily was in Jack's car driving through the iron gates.

"I'm sorry for leaving you to the wolves like that," Jack told her. "Tom Carlton is an old family friend and he had some business to discuss with me before he left town. Unfortunately, it took a lot longer than I'd expected."

"It's okay," she told him, because he seemed genuinely concerned. "I liked your family. They're not at all what I expected."

He glanced over at her. "Should I ask what you expected?"

"I don't know. I guess I didn't expect them to be so…so nice to me. I mean given who they are and who I am and…and the circumstances."

His expression darkened. "They're just people, Lily. As for the circumstances, you didn't exactly make the baby on your own. We both did. If they were going to be upset with anyone, it would be with me."

"But—"

"But they're not upset. The truth is I think my mother is excited. She's been wanting a grandchild for years. I can't tell you the number of times I've heard her complaining that her friends are all grandmothers two and three times over and she doesn't have even one."

"Yes, I think I did hear her mention something about that." Which had surprised Lily. "And she wanted to know what colors I was going to do the nursery in."

"Speaking of that, we haven't talked about where we're going to live. I know you have your apartment and I'm sure it's nice. But it doesn't look like it'd be big enough for three of us."

He was being so tactful, she thought. She knew her one-bedroom apartment was small. She'd already put in a request for a two-bedroom in anticipation of the baby. But she had been hoping to get a house, something with a yard.

"My house has more room and I thought, at least for now, we could live there. Then if you want to find or build something else after the baby comes, we can do that."

Talk of moving to Jack's house brought everything home again. She was marrying Jack Cartwright. She was moving to his home. She could feel the panic setting in again.

"If you'd like, we can swing by the place and you can take a look at it, see if there's anything you want to change."

"That's okay. I'm sure the house will be fine."

"But don't you want to at least see it first—"

"Maybe another time. I'm feeling a little tired." And more than a little worried about whether she was making the right decision—not only for her and the baby, but for Jack, too.

At the sound of Lily's sigh, Jack looked across the seat at her. She had her head tipped back and her eyes were closed. He didn't doubt that she was exhausted. What had started out as a casual brunch had turned into a marathon of wedding plans. Of course, he probably should have known that once they had agreed to have the wedding at the house that the woman would turn into a drill sergeant. Sandra Cartwright was not one to do things in half measures. When he'd walked into the library and seen the glazed look in Lily's eyes he'd known he had to get her out of there.

She'd been a real trooper, he thought as he took the car out onto the interstate. He'd known she'd been nervous, that she'd had misgivings about marrying him. He'd had a few misgivings of his own, he admitted. As his father had pointed out, marriage was tough under ideal circumstances. Their circumstances were anything but ideal. The consensus was that people should marry for love. His parents had. So had a couple of his friends. He and Lily didn't love one another.

But there was something there—chemistry, attraction, and...and something more. In the four days since he'd spotted her outside the counselor's office at Eastwick Cares and learned she was pregnant with his child, that *something* had grown inside him. He cared about her. And not just because of the baby, he admitted. From the way she'd looked at him when he'd come into the library, he wondered if she had felt it, too.

She gasped.

Jack jerked his attention over to Lily. When he saw her rubbing her hand over her stomach, he felt his heart stop a moment. "What's wrong? Is it the baby?"

She looked over at him with those ghost-blue eyes. "Nothing's wrong. And yes, it's the baby. Our son or daughter is kicking again."

Jack swallowed hard. He looked down at her belly and felt the full impact of her words. Their son or daughter. The life growing inside her was a real person. In four months' time he would be holding his child in his arms. A tiny boy or girl whom he was responsible for. A tiny boy or girl who would call him Daddy. He looked up at Lily once more. "Does it hurt? The kicking, I mean."

"I wouldn't say it hurts. It's more uncomfortable than anything. Although I have to admit, those kicks are getting harder as the baby gets bigger."

He turned his attention back to the road. "Is there anything you can do for it?"

She laughed and Jack was struck at the lightness of the sound. It was the first time he'd heard her laugh, he realized. Even the night they'd spent together, she hadn't laughed. There had been desire and passion and even some sadness he'd detected beneath her surface. But there had been no laughter. "Did I say something funny?" he asked, hoping to hear her laugh again.

"Being pregnant isn't like the flu, Jack. The only cure is when the baby is born. But until then, ice cream seems to be the only thing that makes him or her settle down."

"Ice cream? The baby likes ice cream?"

"I think so," she said, a smile in her voice. "Or maybe it's me. All I know is that when our little soccer player starts kicking, I haul out the carton of butter pecan ice cream and once I start shoveling it down, the kicking stops."

Jack laughed. "So our kid likes butter pecan ice cream, huh?"

"Looks that way."

"How does he or she feel about chocolate fudge?" he asked and flipped on his turning signal.

"I don't know. Why?" she asked, sitting up straighter as he took the next exit.

"There's this old-fashioned ice cream parlor not far from here. I thought we'd stop and let our little one decide if he or she is a butter pecan fan like Mom or a chocolate fudge fan like Dad."

It turned out the baby liked butter pecan mixed with chocolate fudge. As far as he was concerned, the mixture was awful, Jack concluded as he turned onto the street leading to Lily's apartment. Lily, on the other hand, had found the combination delicious. And he had felt as though he'd made it over a hurdle because she had been more relaxed with him. So he'd picked up a pint of each to take back to her apartment in the hope that the mood would continue. Once again, he thought of the ring in his pocket.

After pulling his car up to the curb of her apartment building and shutting off the engine, he went around and opened Lily's door. He offered her his hand.

"Thanks," she murmured.

"No problem," he told her as he shut her door. He retrieved the bag with the ice cream from the floor of the back seat.

"I'll take that," she said. "You don't have to come upstairs with me."

Ignoring her, Jack shut the door. "My mother and Grandmother Cartwright taught me always to show a lady to her door."

For a moment, he thought she was going to argue, but then she decided against it, evidently realizing he had no intention of being swayed. Opening the door to the brick four-plex, she preceded him into the building and up the stairs to the second floor. He'd already expressed his concern about her climbing the stairs and she'd assured him the exercise was good for her and the baby.

When he reached the door of her apartment, she unlocked it, then turned to face him. "Thank you, Jack. I really did like your family."

"And they liked you," he told her because it was true.

"Well, then I guess I'll talk to you later."

He held up the bag of ice cream. "I think I'd better put this in the freezer."

"That's okay, I can take that—"

"Lily, I want to come inside." She had yet to invite him inside her apartment, meeting him at the door each time he'd arrived. He knew she was uncomfortable. He didn't blame her. But at some point, they had to get past the awkwardness.

"I really am tired, Jack."

"I promise not to stay long." When she hesitated, he told her, "This time next week, you're going to be my wife." He stroked her cheek with his fingers. "I'm not expecting anything from you. I just think it would be a good idea if we at least reached a point where we don't feel uncomfortable with one another before we get married."

"I know you're right," she said. "But it's not like we're strangers."

"No, we're not. We were drawn to each other for a reason that night and we made a child together. If this marriage is going to work, we're going to have to learn to trust one another."

"I do trust you, Jack. I'm just worried about whether or not we're doing the right thing by getting married."

"We are," he assured her and held up the bag of ice cream. "But if I don't get this in the freezer soon, we're going to have a whole other set of problems."

"The kitchen's right through there," she told him. "Excuse me for a minute."

No doubt the bathroom was calling again, he decided. While she was gone, he took the opportunity to study her home. The place was small, smaller than he'd suspected, he realized as he made the short trek to the kitchen and put the ice cream in the freezer. It was neat, clean and colorful. Lily liked bright colors. He hadn't known that about her. But given the orange print curtains and the dish towels on the counter, the lady surrounded herself with brightness.

She also liked fresh flowers, he noted, spying the arrangement of daisies on the kitchen table and the roses on the coffee table in the living room. Like the kitchen, the living room was small, but bright and cheery. There were lots of homey touches—an afghan on the end of the couch, shelves of books ranging from the latest Sandra Brown thriller to technical books on psychology. There were groupings of candlesticks and books on art and gardening. She liked the Impressionists, he decided, as he checked out two Monet prints. She'd made the place a home.

The only thing that he found missing were photographs. Unlike his and his parents' homes, there were no photographs scattered about the apartment. There were no snapshots of a young Lily on Santa's knee. None of her smiling and showing a gap where she'd lost her first tooth. No pictures of a teenaged Lily dressed for the prom. The absence of any family photos told him more about her than anything else he'd learned via background checks and talks with her. It also caused a tightening in his chest for the young Lily who had grown up without the one thing every child deserved—a family. And along with his aching for her, he couldn't help but feel admiration.

"I'm sorry to take so long," she said as she returned to the room.

Jack turned at the sound of her voice. "No problem," he told her and had to keep himself from going to her and taking her in his arms. "I was just checking out your artwork. I see you like Monet."

"Yes. Degas, too. Someday I've promised myself I'm going to make it to Paris and spend a week in the Louvre."

"You don't have to wait for someday. We can go after the wedding next week. We *are* entitled to a honeymoon," he said and walked over to her. He took her hands in his. "What do you say?"

"I…what about work? We can't just take off."

"I'll clear my schedule and I'm sure you can get some time off from the agency. So, shall I book us some flights?"

"I don't think so," she said and tugged her fingers free. She walked across the room. "I wouldn't be comfortable traveling now…not before the baby comes."

"Then maybe we'll go next spring. April in Paris is beautiful. And when it rains, you can smell the chestnut trees. How does that sound?"

"It sounds lovely," she told him. "Would you like something to drink? I have water, iced tea and soda. I'm afraid I don't have any wine."

"Iced tea would be great." When she disappeared into the kitchen, he slipped his hand into his pocket and fingered the ring box. She'd grown up without family, without having anyone she could rely on but herself. He didn't ever want her to be alone again. He would be her family, he and their baby.

"Here we go," she said as she returned to the room carrying a tray with two glasses, a pitcher, a dish of lemons and a bowl with sweetener.

"Here, let me get that," Jack said, and, taking the tray from her, placed it on the table.

"I wasn't sure if you liked sugar or sweetener. So I brought both." She poured them each a glass and handed him his.

Jack took the glass from her and set it down on the table. "Lily, I don't want tea."

She paused, set down the other glass.

"Would you come sit for a minute?" he asked and patted the seat next to him on the couch.

She did as he asked. "Is there something wrong? Listen, if you've changed your mind about getting married—"

Jack placed his finger over her lips. "I haven't changed my mind. I wanted to give you this." He took the ring box from his pocket and opened it. She gasped at the sight of the antique emerald-cut diamond ring set in the platinum band.

Her blue eyes shot up from the ring to his face. "Jack, I told you I didn't need an engagement ring."

"I know you did. But this isn't just any engagement ring. It's been in my family for nearly two hundred years and it's said that all the women who've worn this ring have enjoyed long, happy marriages."

"Jack, I can't—"

"It belonged to my grandmother and has been passed on to the oldest male descendant in each generation. My mother was an only child and I'm her male descendant, so it came to me, to give to my bride. Since you're going to be my bride, I'd like you to wear it."

"Jack, I can't. It's not right. This is meant to be worn by the woman you lo—"

"It's meant to be worn by the woman I've asked to be my wife. I'm asking you to be my wife, Lily." He took it from the box and held it out to her. "Will you wear it? For me? For our baby?"

For a moment, he thought she was going to refuse. Then she held out her left hand to him.

He slipped the ring onto her finger and it fitted as though it were made for her. Maybe there was something to the Irish mysticism on his mother's side of the family, he thought, because the ring looked right on her finger. It felt right.

"It's beautiful," she told him as she stared at the ring. She met his gaze. "I promise to take care of it."

"I know you will."

"It's getting late," she said and stood.

"Right," he said and walked with her to the door. "I'll call you in the morning," he told her and before she could say anything, he leaned in and kissed her. It was just a brush of lips, no open mouth, no hunger and passion. Yet long after he had left the building, got into his car and was heading home, he could still taste her on his lips.

* * *

Long after Jack had left, Lily continued to lean against the door. Bringing her hand to her mouth, she brushed her fingers along her lips where Jack's lips had touched hers. Unlike the kisses they'd shared that night at the ball, this one had been gentle, loving. It had been a kiss of giving, of promise.

He was marrying her because of the baby, she reminded herself. As she lowered her hand, the diamond in the ring caught and reflected the light. Lifting her hand, Lily stared at it. He'd given her his grandmother's ring.

His grandmother's ring.

It didn't mean anything. It was for the baby, she kept telling herself. But she couldn't shut out Jack's face, the way he had looked at her, his deep blue eyes filled with warmth, with caring. She closed her eyes to block out the image, but he was still there. She could hear his voice, his words echoing in her ears.

It's said that all the women who've worn this ring have enjoyed long, happy marriages.

It belonged to my grandmother…to give to my bride….

I'm asking you to be my wife, Lily. Will you wear it? For me? For our baby?

Opening her eyes, she stared down at the ring again. She had wondered many times how she would feel on this day. A wonderful man, a man who was handsome, kind and generous, a man of integrity, had asked her to be his wife. He'd slid an heirloom ring on her finger and asked her to marry him.

She should be happy. Her baby was going to have everything she could ever have wanted for it—a loving father, a real family. Her child would never be lonely or alone.

She thought of all that the ring symbolized. It didn't feel the way she had thought it would, Lily realized, and swiped at the tears sliding down her cheek. Instead of feeling happy, she felt sadder than she had in a long time.

How could you have been so foolish, Lily? After all these years how could you let yourself get sucked in by the fairy tale?

Because that was just what she had done, she admitted. Sensible, practical Lily Miller, the woman who had lived her life without blinders, the woman who never deluded herself, had done just that. She had thought that when this day happened, when a man placed a ring on her finger and asked her to be his wife, that the man who had put it there would have done so because he loved her.

Five

"While Johanna has made considerable progress since she first started counseling at Eastwick Cares, she continues to exhibit trust issues," Lily said as she dictated notes from her last session. "These trust issues are most likely rooted in her sense of abandonment following her parents' divorce."

She'd seen it dozens of times, Lily admitted as she looked over her case notes. Too often when a couple divorced it was the children who came away with the most scars. She'd lost count of the times that children like twelve-year-old Johanna Stevenson blamed themselves. And as the family unit dissolved and the parents spent less and less time with their children in order to resume their own social lives, the children lost their sense of security. As a result, children like Johanna Stevenson felt unwanted, unloved and in the way.

Lily thought of her baby and knew she didn't want her child ever to feel that way. It was the reason she and Jack had agreed to get married in the first place—to provide their baby with a family. Unlike her, her child would grow up knowing it was loved, feeling secure.

"Knock, knock," Felicity Farnsworth said as she stuck her head inside the door. "Oh, good. I was hoping I'd catch you before you left for lunch," she said and breezed inside carrying a white zippered dress bag.

"Felicity, I wasn't expecting you," Lily told her as she stood.

"I know you weren't, but I left you a couple of messages and when I didn't hear back from you, I figured you were too busy to come to me. So I decided to come to you instead."

"I'm sorry. I did get your messages, but I've been kind of busy," Lily offered even though that was only half true. She hadn't called primarily because she felt like a fraud having Jack and his family going to so much trouble when the marriage wasn't a real one.

"Not a problem," Felicity told her, her green eyes lighting up her face. Once again dressed in black, she had a bright blue butterfly pin perched on her shoulder. A smaller version was anchored in her choppy blond hair. She smiled. "That's why you hired me—to take care of all the details for you. And this," she said, indicating the garment bag that bore the name of a bridal boutique, "is a very important detail."

"Felicity," Lily began. "Now's not a good time. I have another appointment due in fifteen minutes."

"Then I promise to be out of here in ten. I just need you to try this on and see if you like it. It's your wedding dress."

"But I don't need a wedding dress." The truth is she hadn't given a thought to buying one. She had just planned on wearing the pale yellow linen suit she'd bought for Easter.

"Every bride needs a wedding dress. And since you're too busy to shop for one, I picked out one I thought you might

like." She hung the bag on the back of the door and began un-
zipping it.

"Really, Felicity. This isn't necessary. I hardly fit the picture of the blushing bride," Lily reminded her, keenly aware
of her protruding stomach.

"Nonsense," Felicity told her. "If only virgin brides were
allowed to wear wedding gowns, there would be very few
wedding gowns sold," she informed her and removed the
dress from the bag.

It was beautiful, Lily thought as she stared at the ivory-
colored silk gown. The style was simple. The off-the-shoulder neckline had small silken rosettes at each shoulder. The
bodice was fitted, then formed an Empire-style waistline that
fell to the floor and would conceal her swollen middle.

"I had to guess at the size," Felicity said as she held the
dress up to Lily. "Do you like it?"

"It's beautiful," Lily said and ran her fingers along the
fabric. Then she spied the tag sewn into the dress—Vera
Wang—and sucked in a breath. She might not know a Vera
Wang from a vintage Dior, but what she did know was that
both were very, very expensive. "Felicity, I can't possibly
wear this."

Felicity's expression fell. "But I thought you liked it."

"I do like it. In fact, I love it. It's one of the most beautiful
dresses I've ever seen. But I can't afford it."

"Oh, that," she said, waving aside the comment. A smile
spread across her face "It's already been taken care of."

Lily frowned. "What do you mean it's been taken care
of?" she asked, even though she suspected she knew—Jack
had been the one to take care of it.

"Mrs. Cartwright had the bill sent to her."

It didn't matter whether it had been Jack or his mother, Lily
thought. "I'm sorry, Felicity. I know she means well, but I

couldn't possibly let her pay for it. And since I can't afford it, I'll just wear something of my own."

Felicity sobered. "Lily, I understand you wanting to pay your own way. Really, I do. I was married once and I went through some rough times financially when it ended. It took me a long time to get back on my feet and I had to do it on my own. So I know all about the need to feel independent and responsible for yourself."

"So you understand why I can't possibly accept the gown."

"What I understand is that you're marrying a very wealthy man and into a very wealthy family. The Cartwrights have a position within the Eastwick community. Whether it's fair or not, people expect a certain level of style from them."

Lily felt a tightening in her chest. "And I certainly don't fit the profile of a wife for Jack Cartwright."

"You do as far as he's concerned. I think you could wear a fig leaf and that man would be happy. In fact, he might like it better if you came in a fig leaf."

Lily laughed, as she was sure Felicity meant her to do. "A fig leaf I can afford."

"But I'm not sure his family would be thrilled with the choice," Felicity pointed out.

"So what am I supposed to do? Just let Sandra spend a fortune on a dress for me?"

"No. You're supposed to let the mother of the man you're going to marry feel that she did something special for you. I know it may seem superficial, but appearances are important to her. She wants to make you feel like you're one of them. And this is her way of doing it. It's important to her that she does this for you. It makes her feel like she's a part of things, that she's not losing her son."

Lily could feel herself relenting. At least she wouldn't have to worry about embarrassing Jack or herself by wearing something that was too common for the woman who was becoming Mrs. Jack Cartwright. "It really is a beautiful dress."

"Yes, it is. And I think it's perfect for you. But you don't have to take my word for it. Why don't you try it on and let's see how it looks. For all we know you could be agonizing over whether or not to accept it as a gift for nothing because you might hate the way it looks on you."

"I doubt that," Lily said as she looked at the dress again.

"I brought a couple of different shoe styles in two sizes because I wasn't sure if you were having any problems with swelling."

Tearing her eyes from the dress, Lily glanced over and saw the shopping bag by the door. "I can't believe you went to all this trouble."

"It's no trouble. It's what I do and I have to confess I love it. Besides, your fiancé made me promise that I would make this wedding as stress-free for you as possible."

"Jack asked you to do that?"

"Mmm-hmm. He said it took some arm-twisting to get you to agree to marry him and he wanted everything to be perfect for you."

Lily swallowed, unsure what to say.

"Come on, let's see how it fits," Felicity said, and after locking the door, she took the dress from Lily and waited for her to undress. Felicity held the dress for Lily to step into. Once she had it on, the other woman pulled up the zipper and then began fussing with the rosettes above each shoulder. When she was satisfied, she stood back. "Oh, Lily," she said, and brought her palms together. Her expression softened. "You look beautiful. And the ivory color, it looks wonderful against your skin. Do you have a mirror anywhere?"

"In the bathroom through there," Lily said, indicating the door at the far side of the office.

"Then come, see for yourself."

Lily went into the bathroom and stared at herself in the mirror. It was the dress. It was beautiful, and it made her look different. She didn't even look pregnant because the design camouflaged her stomach. The off-the-shoulder neckline also exposed more of her than she was used to, including more cleavage, she realized, pressing her hand to her chest. She had never had a big bust and at best, her cleavage had been attained with the help of miracle bras. But her stomach hadn't been the only thing that had grown since her pregnancy. And while she would never be as full-figured as Felicity, she definitely had more curves. "You don't think it shows a little too much?"

"I think it looks perfect on you. Hang on, let me get the shoes." She disappeared into the other room and came back with the shopping bag, then she took out a box that contained a pair of ivory satin pumps with kitten heels. "Let's try these."

Lily slipped her feet into the shoes. They fitted perfectly. The pointed tips peeked out from beneath the skirt.

"How do they feel?" Felicity asked as she stood.

"They feel great."

"And they look wonderful with the dress." She smiled again. "You're going to make a beautiful bride, Lily. I can't wait to see Jack's face when he sees you walking down the aisle."

Lily sobered. She met Felicity's eyes in the mirror. "You don't have to pretend. I'm sure you know this marriage isn't a love match, and that the only reason Jack is marrying me is because I'm pregnant."

"Are you sure about that?"

"What do you mean?" Lily asked as she slipped off the shoes and took off the wedding dress. She handed the gown to Felicity and retrieved her own clothes.

"I mean that I saw the way Jack was looking at you the

other day and it wasn't the way a man looks at a woman he's marrying out of duty."

"You're mistaken."

"Am I?" Felicity asked as she returned the wedding gown to the garment bag and zipped it closed. "I've been in this business for quite some time now and I've seen my share of weddings. Usually I can tell the couples whose marriage is being done out of duty or as a business merger from the ones who are marrying because they love one another. I would have sworn you and Jack were the latter."

The knock at the door, signaling her next appointment, saved Lily from responding. But as she bid Felicity goodbye and ushered her next client in, she couldn't help wishing that Felicity were right.

Jack waited impatiently at the front of the garden for the wedding ceremony to begin. Now he knew why people eloped, he thought. The stress leading up to the wedding was enough to cause a body to have a heart attack. Or maybe it was simply the fact that he didn't quite trust Lily not to run. An eager bride she wasn't. Despite her signature on the prenuptial agreement and the trusts he'd set up for her and the baby, he wasn't going to be able to relax until he had that wedding band on her finger.

"I still can't believe you're getting married," Scott Falcon told him in a low voice as he stood beside him to fulfill the duties of the best man.

"Believe it, because it's happening," Jack told him. He glanced at his watch and frowned. "Or at least it will be happening if they ever get the ceremony started."

Scott chuckled beside him. "Never thought I'd see the day when a female tied you up in knots. This Lily must be pretty special."

"She is," Jack said. And she was. In the short time he'd

known her, each day he'd learned something new about her that told him just how special she was.

"You do realize that by getting married you're crushing the dreams of half the single women in Eastwick, not to mention the mothers who were hoping to snag you for their daughters?"

"Then it's a good thing they've got your shoulder to cry on, isn't it?"

Scott smiled. "Always happy to help out a friend."

And he was a good friend, Jack thought. Pals since grade school, he and Scott had shared adventures, pranks and an occasional girlfriend over the years. Like him, Scott's family had been among the first settlers in Connecticut and had amassed a sizeable fortune in real estate. A person could hardly walk down a street in Eastwick without seeing the Falcon logo somewhere on it. Scott had been among the very few people who had understood his decision to marry Lily and offered his support.

"Your mother and Felicity did a nice job," Scott remarked.

"Yes, they did," Jack responded. Somehow the two women had pulled it off. He didn't know how much it had cost nor did he care. All that had mattered to him was that they'd put the wedding together in less than a week. He knew from his conversation with Lily that they had found her a gown and shoes. He also knew that Lily had been uncomfortable and reluctant to accept the expensive attire as a gift from his mother. That she had done so, he suspected, had been a concession on her part because she had feared embarrassing him. Of course, it had never crossed his mother's mind that Lily might object to such a gift. As usual, Sandra had bulldozed ahead and set out to create the perfect wedding for him and Lily.

From the looks of things, she had succeeded. Even the weather had cooperated with his mother's plans to hold the ceremony outdoors. The temperature was mild and sunshine had replaced the rain that had plagued Eastwick off and on for the past two weeks. He'd caught a peek of the sprawling patio on the south side of the house that had been transformed for the wedding reception. Twinkling lights had been strung from the trees. More flowers decorated the tables and entrances. Two ice sculptures had been placed on tables on either side of the patio. The six-tiered cake decorated with what looked like real flowers sat in the center of one table. He'd counted at least a dozen food stations, including three types of pasta, a prime rib station, grilled shrimp and salmon. Bars had been set up on either end of the patio and he could have sworn there was enough wait staff on hand for a hundred-seat restaurant.

Yes, his mother and Felicity Farnsworth had outdone themselves, he thought as he looked around him. In addition to the reception area, they had managed to turn the garden of his parents' estate into a small wedding chapel. Everywhere he looked there were peach and white roses and lilies. Vases and urns of the blossoms had been placed on the altar, on the piano, at the entrance to the gardens. A white runner formed an aisle between the three dozen chairs arranged in rows on either side. White ribbons with more roses and lilies anchored posts at the end of each row. From where he was standing, it looked as if every seat was filled. He shifted his gaze back to the altar where the minister stood waiting to make him and Lily man and wife.

He was nervous, Jack admitted to himself. Except for that one time years ago, he hadn't given much thought to marriage. Not that he'd ruled it out. He hadn't. He liked women. He liked everything about them—the way they looked, the way they smelled, the way they were strong and soft at the same time, the way they were different from men. He enjoyed women. And they seemed to enjoy him. He just hadn't expected that when he decided to marry he'd find himself standing here wondering whether his bride was going to be a no-show.

When he had suggested he and Lily marry, it had seemed so simple. They had a baby on the way, a child that needed both parents. But now that the day was finally here, he couldn't help worrying that he had pushed Lily too hard. Oh, he'd known she had reservations and he didn't blame her. Marriage was a big undertaking and neither of them had had much time to prepare for it. But he was positive that marrying was the right thing for them to do. He'd meant what he'd told Lily. He wanted to be a real father in every way and that meant being a full-time father, not shuffling their child back and forth between its parents. No, he wanted his baby to have what he and his sisters had had—a loving home with both parents. And although the stigma that society had once imposed upon a child born outside of marriage no longer applied, he didn't want his child or Lily ever to encounter cruelty from the small-minded individuals who would see the baby's birth as a sin. He wanted to protect the baby and Lily and the best way to do that was through marriage.

But he couldn't shake the feeling she was going to bolt. He knew she was having second thoughts—probably third and fourth thoughts—about going through with the wedding. It hadn't taken a giant leap to recognize the signs. She had avoided him at every turn during the past week. Just getting her to look over the documents he'd had drawn up providing her and their baby each with a trust fund had taken some major arm-twisting. It had also bothered him that she had insisted on keeping her apartment until the lease ran out despite his offer to buy out the lease. He hadn't pushed it because he was already worried about the stress she was under and didn't want to do anything that would endanger her health or the baby's. Maybe once the wedding was over and they were living under the same roof, she would grow more comfortable with him and the idea of them being married, he told himself.

"I heard Courtney moved back from New York," Scott remarked.

Dragging his attention to his friend, Jack said, "Yeah. She came home a couple of weeks ago."

"She going to stay?"

"I don't know." Jack looked over at Scott. Tall like him, Scott was the opposite of him in appearance. Where his own hair was dark and his eyes blue, Scott was blond and his eyes were brown. Like him, Scott had a real appreciation of women, had found himself in more than one woman's marital sights and had become a master at escaping any serious commitment. He'd been a fixture at the Cartwright house when they'd been growing up and had shared in Jack's own annoyance with his two younger sisters. Jack hadn't given much thought to his baby sister's return home and hadn't realized Scott had either. So he asked, "What makes you ask?"

"No reason," Scott said and looked away.

They fell silent and Jack's thoughts returned once more to Lily. He looked at his watch again. As the minutes ticked by, he grew more and more anxious. "You got the ring?" he asked Scott.

Scott patted his pocket. "Right here." He paused. "I've never seen you so nervous before. You sure about this, Jack?"

"I'm sure," he told his friend, because he knew he was doing what was best for everyone. Now all they needed was the bride.

When the violinist began playing, Jack turned and looked at the end of the aisle where his sister Courtney stood under the arbor of flowers. Dressed in a peach-colored dress and holding a small bouquet of peach roses and lilies, she started down the aisle with a smile on her face. When Courtney was about midway down the aisle, his sister Elizabeth stepped under the arbor. Since Lily hadn't been able to think of anyone to ask to be her maid of honor, his youngest sister had volunteered herself for the job. Lily, apparently not wanting Elizabeth to feel left out, had suggested both of his sisters serve as attendants. It was a decision that had pleased both his sisters and his mother—and him because he wanted Lily to feel that she was truly a part of his family now. Once his sisters had reached the altar and taken their places, the first notes of the wedding march rang out.

Both anxious and excited, Jack turned his gaze once more to the entrance at the rear of the gardens. This is it, he told himself as he waited for Lily to appear beneath the flower arbor and walk down the aisle to become his wife. Several seconds went by, but there was no Lily. The first notes of the bridal march were played again. And still there was no Lily.

Jack tensed, his first thought that he'd been right to worry. He'd pushed her too hard, and, just as he'd feared, she'd decided not to go through with the wedding. His second thought was that something had happened to her, that maybe she'd slipped on the stone floor inside the house and was hurt. It was that last thought, imagining Lily hurt, that had him starting to leave the altar to find her.

"Hang on," Scott whispered, gripping his arm before he could go. He motioned for him to look at the rear of the guest seats where Felicity was signaling to him to give her a minute. The blonde disappeared, evidently going through the side door of the house to where Lily was supposed to be waiting.

Jack could hear the murmurs among the guests, the shifting in their seats, and he saw the anxious look on his mother's face. Damn it. They just should have eloped, he reasoned. If they had, Lily wouldn't have had time to think about changing her mind.

And if she has changed her mind? What are you going to do?

He was going to change it back, he told himself. He couldn't afford not to. Looking at his watch, he decided to give Felicity five minutes and then he was going to do just that.

"Relax," Scott told him. "She probably broke a nail or got a run in her stocking. You know how women are about those things."

He did know how women were. A broken nail or a run in a stocking would have sent his mother and his sister Courtney and probably half the women he'd dated into a frenzy. But not Lily. Lily was not most women. He'd sensed that the night of the ball. It was one of the reasons, he knew, that he'd given a woman whose name he didn't know the key to his hotel room. It was also the reason that he hadn't been able to get her out of his mind since that night.

Granted, the only reason he had suggested they get married was because she was pregnant with his child. He'd never been a man to shirk responsibility. He had no intention of doing so now. Lily and the baby were his responsibility now. But if he was going to be completely honest with himself he didn't find the idea unappealing. There had been something special between them that night at the ball—something that went beyond the good sex. Whatever that something was, it would be enough to start with because he didn't intend to lose her again.

She couldn't go through with it, Lily told herself as she stood in front of the vanity in the powder room of the Cartwright mansion. She stared at the woman in the mirror. That woman looked like a real bride. The wedding gown was beautiful. So were the shoes. Her hair had been swept up into an elegant French twist with wisps arranged around her face. Courtney had performed miracles with the paints and polishes and brushes, making Lily's skin look creamy, her eyes bright and her cheekbones those of a model. She touched the strand of pearls with the diamond clasp at her throat and noted the matching earrings. Both were wedding gifts from Jack. "For my bride," he'd told her when he'd given them to her the previous evening.

Wedding gifts for a bride. Even the bouquet of white roses and lilies looked as if they belonged to a bride. No question about it. The woman looking back at her in the mirror certainly looked like a real, honest-to-goodness bride.

Only she wasn't a real bride. She was a fake.

And she absolutely, positively couldn't go through with the wedding.

When Jack had suggested that they get married, it had all seemed to make sense. After all, he was the baby's father and she had wanted her baby to have a real home with two parents. It had also made sense when he'd told her that shuffling the child between the two of them wouldn't work. She'd seen firsthand how tough shuffling between parents could be on a child. She hadn't wanted that for her baby. And as Jack Cartwright's wife, she could be assured that her child would have the loving home she had never had.

Only now that the day was here, she simply could not go through with it. She didn't love Jack Cartwright and he didn't love her. And when two people got married it should be because they loved one another, not because their hormones had run amok one night and resulted in a pregnancy. While she understood Jack feeling he needed to take responsibility, he didn't need to marry her to do it. The man deserved a happy life with someone he loved. So did she. They could still love their baby, be good parents and provide a stable, loving home without making such a colossal mistake. Because going through with this marriage would be just that, she reasoned— a colossal mistake.

The first notes of the bridal march started and panic began to swim in her blood. She had to get out of here. Maybe she could slip out the powder room, make it out the front door and hightail it to the main road and try to find a taxi. Jack would understand. Shoot, he'd probably be relieved, she told herself as she turned and moved as quickly as she could with a ten-pound ball around her middle. She had almost reached the door when it burst open and in flew Felicity.

"Lily, didn't you hear your cue?"

"Yes, I did. Felicity, I—"

"Where's your bouquet?" she demanded and swept her gaze over the room to the dressing table. She scooped it up, stuck it in Lily's hands. After fussing with her hair for a moment, Felicity stepped back. "You look gorgeous. And wait until you see your groom. The man should live in a tux."

"Felicity—"

"Listen, there's your cue again," Felicity told her.

Lily's hands began to shake, but evidently Felicity didn't notice that the roses and lilies were trembling like the leaves on an aspen in a windstorm. "I don't think I can do this."

"Sure you can," Felicity insisted and straightened the skirt of her gown. She gave her a quick hug and a smile. "Just take a deep breath and think of Jack." And before she could say another word, Felicity flew out the door as quickly as she had blown in.

The first notes of the bridal march started for the third time and Lily couldn't move. She stood frozen in the powder room and wished she was Samantha from the old *Bewitched* TV show so she could wiggle her nose and disappear. She was still standing there wondering if she was going to be sick when the door to the powder room opened again. Only this time it was Jack who came in.

Her first crazy thought was that Felicity had been right. The man really should live in a tux. The black jacket made his

houlders look broad, his height towering. His black hair was
hick, his blue eyes as dark as steel. His jawline was strong,
is mouth almost elegant. There was something solid and
commanding and, at the same time, dangerous about him—
he very things that had drawn her to him that night at the ball.

"I wasn't sure if you remembered to check your calendar
his morning," he said, his voice casual. "But according to
mine, we're supposed to be getting married right about now."

"I didn't forget," Lily told him. Taking a deep breath, she
looked up at him and into his eyes. "I'm sorry, Jack. I know
ow much trouble you and your family have gone to, but I
an't go through with it. I just can't."

"I see."

I see?

It wasn't the response she had expected. In truth, she had
xpected him to be angry. After all, the man had gone to a
reat deal of trouble and expense to arrange the wedding. He
ad at least three dozen family members and friends sitting
utside waiting to see him take her as his bride. He'd even
iven her his grandmother's ring. No question about it, Jack
Cartwright had every right to be downright furious with her.
Only instead of being angry, he took the bridal bouquet she
vas clutching in her still unsteady hands and placed it on the
ressing table. Then he took her by the hand and led her to
he bench by the wall.

"Why don't we sit down a minute?"

She did as he suggested and said, "I'm not going to change
ny mind, Jack. I'm sorry, but I simply can't go through with
. I can't marry you."

"All right," he told her. He sat down beside her, took her other
and and held it in his. "So is there any particular reason you
on't want to marry me?" he asked calmly. And before she could
nd her voice, he continued, "Is it my nose? I broke it playing

football in college and it never did heal quite right. Maybe yo
don't want to be married to a man with an ugly nose."

"There's nothing wrong with your nose. It's beautiful."

"The hair then. You probably noticed that I'm starting
get a few gray hairs right around the temples. I know son
women find that a turn-off—"

"There's nothing wrong with your hair. It looks great. Yc
look great," she insisted.

"Hmm. It isn't because I'm a lawyer, is it? I mean, I'v
heard all the lawyer jokes and I know we're not the most po
ular people."

He was deliberately being absurd to calm her, she realize
"It's not any of those things. You're handsome, charmin
kind and one of the nicest men I've ever known."

Jack winced. "You make me sound like my grandfather. I
much prefer you thought I was sexy."

Her lips twitched. "I do think you're sexy—which you a
ready know. Otherwise, we wouldn't be in this situation."

"But we are in this situation," he said. "In four month
we're going to be parents. And I thought we agreed that f
the baby's sake, we should get married."

"I know we did. But we were wrong. *I* was wrong," she to
him and, unable to sit still, she stood. "I should never hav
agreed to it. It's crazy to think this marriage would ever wor
I don't know what I was thinking to have agreed to it in th
first place."

"You were thinking about what's best for our baby." H
rose and came up behind her. "Our baby needs a mother an
a father, Lily."

"He or she will have a mother and a father," she insiste
"We don't have to be married to be good parents. Lots of co
ples raise children without being husband and wife."

"We already covered this, Lily. Neither of us wants o

child to grow up being shuffled from one house to the other, splitting time between Mom and Dad on holidays and weekends. I want our baby to have a real home, a real family. I want our baby to have what you never had. I thought you did, too."

She hated that he was right. She did want that type of home for her baby. She wanted the picture-perfect home for her baby that she'd always longed for, but had never known. The kind of home she'd read about in books when she was a girl where children were loved and felt secure. She wanted to sit at the dinner table together as a family, to decorate the Christmas tree as a family, to bake cookies together and have picnics in the backyard. She wanted her child to have a family and never, ever feel alone as she had. "I do want those things. Making sure my baby feels loved and secure it's…it's what's most important to me."

"To me, too. And we can make sure our baby is loved and secure by providing him or her with a real home with both of its parents." He placed his hands on her shoulders, turned her to face him. "Our child can have that, Lily. All you have to do is marry me."

He made it sound so easy, so logical. But it wasn't. She knew it wasn't. "What about love, Jack? You know you don't love me." And that was the problem. She couldn't let go of the idea that she wanted to marry for love.

"And you don't love me. But we both love our baby," he pointed out.

"But what if that's not enough? We'll be trapped in a loveless marriage."

"I don't see marriage to you as a trap. I see it as a gift. I'll be getting a smart, beautiful wife and the mother of my child."

"And love? Don't you even believe in love, Jack?"

"There are all kinds of love. Love of family, love of a parent and child, love of a friend."

"What about love between a man and a woman, a husband and wife? Don't you believe in that?" she asked. "Don't you want that?"

"I believe that there are some people, like my parents, who find that kind of connection. I don't know if it starts out that way or if it's something that grows over time out of respect and caring for one another. What I do believe in is the power of hormones between a man and a woman," he told her. He drew his fingertip down her cheek and Lily could feel her already nervous stomach flutter at his touch. "I still want you, Lily. And I think you want me."

She swallowed past the knot that seemed to have lodged in her throat. "You're talking about meaningless sex."

"I'm talking about desire, passion. It's still there between us. Just like it was that night."

It was true, Lily admitted silently. The pull between them that had drawn her to him that night and that had led her to breaking all her personal rules by sleeping with him was still there. In fact, it was even stronger now that she'd gotten to know him better. "What if desire isn't enough to make it work?"

"It's more than a lot of people have," he said. "I think we owe it to our baby to at least try."

Once again he made the whole thing sound so simple, so logical. Jack was a good man, an honest man and she had no doubt that he would be a good father to their child. Yet, it felt wrong to start any marriage this way.

"It's your call, Lily. You know how I feel, that I think the two of us marrying is the right thing to do for our baby's sake. So what's it going to be? Should I go out there and tell everyone that the bride has changed her mind and there isn't going to be a wedding after all? Or do I go out there and tell the minister to get the show on the road before the ice sculptures melt?"

She took a deep breath and met his gaze. "Tell the minister to get the show on the road," she told him.

"You won't be sorry, Lily. I promise."

She certainly hoped Jack was right, she thought as he disappeared out the door. When she heard the bridal march start once again, Lily picked up her bouquet. As she exited the powder room and started toward the garden where she would pledge to become Jack Cartwright's wife, she prayed she wasn't making a mistake that both of them would live to regret.

Six

As he returned to his position at the altar, Jack didn't miss the looks and whispers that followed him. He glanced over at the front row on the right where his mother sat on the edge of her seat, her white gloves clasped tightly in her hands, a worried expression on her face. His father met his gaze and when Jack nodded, John sat back and took his wife's hand.

"Everything okay?" Scott asked in a low voice.

"Everything's fine."

Despite what he told his friend, he wasn't at all sure everything was fine. Lily had looked terrified when he'd found her in that powder room. She'd been hit by a major case of cold feet. He couldn't say he blamed her. Her entire world was being turned upside-down. Not only was she pregnant with his baby, she was marrying a man she knew very little about and she was becoming a member of the Cartwright family. In his opinion neither of those things would inspire much confidence. He wasn't sure which was more daunting—marrying him or marrying into his family because, as much as he loved his family, he knew being a Cartwright wasn't always easy. A lot of expectations and responsibilities came with the family name and the fortune. He'd had his entire life to learn to deal with both. Lily had had less than two weeks.

When the first chords of the bridal march sounded once again, he stared at the entrance. Despite the fact that she'd agreed to go through with the wedding, he wasn't at all confident that she would. And just when he thought she had decided against marrying him after all, there she was—standing at the entrance beneath the flowered arbor.

She was beautiful, he thought as she stepped up to the end of the white runner. He'd heard the old wives' tale about women who were pregnant having a glow about them. He'd never put much stock in it, never had reason to before now, he guessed. But Lily was living proof that it was true. She glowed. She'd put her hair up in some kind of twist thing, but little pieces had slipped free and fell around her face. The effect of the deep red strands against that creamy skin was striking. And just as he had done when he'd seen her for the first time at the ball five months ago, he was unable to take his eyes off her. There was something about her, something beyond her beauty and the physical chemistry that drew him to her, just as it had drawn him to her that long-ago night.

He could see the stress swirling in those ghost-blue eyes of hers as she started down the aisle. He didn't miss the slight remor in the hands that were holding the bouquet either. When she finally reached him, she looked as though she still might turn and run. So he reached out and caught her hand. Judging by the Reverend Lawrence's frown, he'd just committed some kind of sin. Evidently touching the bride at this point in the ceremony was a big no-no.

Too bad, Jack thought. Rules or no rules, if holding her hand made any of this easier for Lily, then that's what he intended to do.

"Dearly beloved, we are gathered here today to join this man and this woman in holy matrimony," the minister began.

Jack could feel three dozen pairs of eyes on his back, watching him, watching her, watching them. He'd shocked his friends and business associates when he'd announced that he was marrying Lily…and that he was going to be a father. He'd known they had had some reservations, but they also knew that when he made up his mind about something, there was no changing it. So they'd wisely kept most of their reservations to themselves. Fortunately, his family had rallied behind him with their support.

"If there be anyone here who knows why these two people should not be joined in wedlock, let them speak now or forever hold their peace."

Lily tensed beside him and he half expected her to object. Wouldn't that be a first? he thought, amused at the image of the bride objecting to her own wedding. Talk about a scandal on top of a scandal. He could just see the headlines in Bunny Baldwin's *Social Diary*. Jack Cartwright's Bride Bolts from Shotgun Wedding. Poor Bunny, the lady must be giving them hell in heaven because she was missing some of the juiciest gossip to hit Eastwick in years.

His thoughts wandering, Jack felt Lily squeezing his hand. Shaking off his musings, he looked down at her, noted the anxious look in her eyes, the twin spots of color on her cheeks. He knew she was trying to tell him something. But what? That she was scared? That she had changed her mind?

"Jack. Jack." The minister repeated his name.

Jack jerked his gaze over to Reverend Lawrence and realized then that he'd missed something.

"Do you, John Ryan Cartwright, take Lily Miller to be you

lawfully wedded wife, for richer, for poorer, in sickness and in health? Do you promise to love her and honor her, forsaking all others until you are parted by death?"

"I do," Jack said firmly.

"Then repeat after me. I, John Ryan Cartwright, do take thee, Lily Miller, to be my wedded wife."

"I, John Ryan Cartwright, do take thee, Lily Miller, to be my wedded wife…"

"For richer, for poorer. In sickness and in health," the minister continued.

"For richer, for poorer, in sickness and in health," Jack repeated.

"I promise to love you and honor you, forsaking all others, until we are parted by death."

Repeating the vow, he never took his eyes from Lily's face as he said, "I promise to love you and honor you, forsaking all others, until we are parted by death."

After Lily repeated the vows to him, the reverend asked for the rings. Jack took the ring from Scott and turned back to face Lily.

"Repeat after me. With this ring, I thee wed."

"With this ring, I thee wed," Jack said and he slid the platinum band onto Lily's finger as he pledged himself to her.

The minister turned to Lily, who took the ring from his sister, then, sliding the ring onto Jack's finger, she said, "With this ring, I thee wed."

Moments later, Reverend Lawrence said, "By the power vested in me, I now pronounce you man and wife. You may kiss the bride."

Jack kissed her. He'd meant for the kiss to be brief, a simple brush of his lips against hers. It was tradition. It was expected and he didn't want to add to Lily's stress by keeping her on display any longer than necessary. But when his mouth touched hers, he lingered. Only for a moment, but long enough for the taste of her to fill his head, long enough for his pulse to begin beating like a jackhammer, long enough for him to remember why they'd found themselves standing before a minister exchanging vows in the first place.

And judging by the look in Lily's eyes, she was remembering, too.

"Ladies and gentlemen," Reverend Lawrence said. "May I present to you Mr. and Mrs. John Ryan Cartwright."

It was done, Jack told himself as he and Lily turned to face the applauding guests. He and Lily were now man and wife. The pianist hit the keys again, and as the joyful tune rang out, he placed Lily's hand on his arm and led her down the aisle.

An hour later, Jack decided he'd had enough. From the look on Lily's face, she had, too. "Excuse me," he told his longtime friend and fellow attorney Dan Granger. "I'd better go rescue Lily before my mother ropes her into joining her bridge club."

"Sure, go ahead," Dan told him. "But, Jack, I hope you won't be too quick to rule out the senate race. With Carlton's group behind you, you'd have a good shot at claiming that seat. And we could certainly use someone like you on Capitol Hill."

"I appreciate that, Dan. But right now, my focus is on my new wife and our family," he explained. While he hadn't ruled out a run for office, after speaking with his father, he wasn't sure he wanted to put Lily through the ordeal. He had absolutely no qualms or reservations about Lily's unplanned pregnancy and their marriage. Nor did he feel anything but pride for where she came from and what she had made of herself. He knew from her comments that her lack of family and knowledge about her heritage bothered her.

"I understand. I shouldn't have even bothered you about

this on your wedding day. We'll talk about it in a week or two. And congratulations again on your marriage."

"Thanks," Jack said, and, after shaking Dan's hand, he headed across the patio to where Lily was standing with his mother and two women he recognized as part of her bridge group.

"Jack, darling," his mother said and beamed as he joined them. "You remember Louise and Pamela from my bridge group, don't you?"

"Yes, of course. Good afternoon, ladies," he said with a bow of his head.

"I was just telling your mother what a beautiful bride you have," the ash-blond Pamela told him.

"Thank you. I happen to think she's beautiful, too," Jack said and he stared directly at Lily. He didn't miss the rush of color to her cheeks. "If you ladies don't mind, I'm going to steal my wife away for a few minutes."

He reached for Lily's hand and as he was hustling her away, he spied his great-aunt Olivia Cartwright heading toward them. "Aunt Olivia at two o'clock. Come on," he said and led her out to the center of the floor.

"Jack, what are you doing?" she asked as he took her in his arms and spun her around the stone patio floor in time to the music.

"Dancing with my wife."

"But why?"

"Because my great-aunt Olivia considers herself the authority on everything from business to marriage to giving birth. Trust me, you don't want her to start offering us advice."

"Oh," she said. "Did you say she was your great-aunt?"

"Yes. My grandmother's older sister." Grateful that the band was playing a slow tune, he held Lily close. It reminded him of the night at the ball when he'd held her in his arms for the first time. Just as on that night she felt soft and silky and as elusive as moonlight. He breathed in her scent, the hint of roses and sunshine and some mysterious scent that was hers alone. She fitted him perfectly and he was keenly aware of the weight of her breasts against his chest, the way her dress swished against his pant legs as they moved their feet in harmony. He was also aware of the roundness of her abdomen pressing against him.

"You have a lot of relatives," she said, her breath whispering against his ear and causing that rapid beat in his pulse again. "What's it like being a part of a big family?"

"Annoying," he told her and tried to shake off his sexual feelings. The last thing Lily needed right now was for him to start making marital demands on her. Besides the fact that she was pregnant, she had had her entire life turned upside down. Now that she was a Cartwright her life would never be the same again. Right or wrong, the name *Cartwright* meant money and power. And while giving his name to her and their child would provide security and protection, it would also subject her to the curiosity, rumors and often the envy of others. Some of it had already started. He'd had a flurry of calls from friends, business acquaintances, members of the country club and even former girlfriends when the news had broken of his impending marriage. He didn't doubt that the gossip mill was working overtime with the scandal of Lily's pregnancy and their marriage. Of course, without Bunny Baldwin and her *Social Diary* to feed the frenzy, it might lose steam quickly. At least he hoped it would. Until then, he intended to shield Lily from it as much as he could.

Easing back, she looked at him. "I'd have thought it would be wonderful to have so many people related to you. You'd never be alone. There would always be someone to share the holidays with, to spend special moments with."

He knew that Lily had spent most of her holidays alone,

the outsider watching foster families celebrating. There was a part of him that ached for the lonely girl she must have been. He couldn't go back and wipe away those unhappy memories, but he promised himself that he would make happy memories for her in the future. "I guess it is pretty nice most of the time—except at times like today when those well-meaning family members, like my mother, insist on getting in your business and hosting receptions like this one so that she can show us off."

"It's not that bad," she told him.

"Shh. Don't let her hear you say that or she'll never let us out of here." Lily smiled and it was the first real smile he'd seen from her all afternoon. Drawing her close, he moved her into a slow spin.

"We're being watched," she told him.

"Ignore them," he said, not wanting to allow anyone to intrude upon the moment. It was the first time she'd come close to relaxing with him since they'd agreed to get married.

"That might be kind of hard to do. Your aunt Olivia is waving a napkin at us. I think she wants us to come over to her."

"She's *our* aunt Olivia now," he informed her. He had indeed seen Aunt Olivia motioning them over. She'd been hard to miss since she was the only eighty-five-year-old woman with Lucille Ball red hair holding a glass of bourbon in one hand and a cane in the other. "You do realize that now that you're a Cartwright, all these annoyingly wonderful relatives are yours now, too—including Aunt Olivia."

"Um, Jack. I think *our* aunt Olivia is getting impatient."

Jack glanced over to where his great-aunt had just slapped her glass down on a table and was insisting the young waiter help her to her feet. "We'd better go see what she wants."

What she wanted was to give them both a lecture on what was necessary to make a marriage work. Since Aunt Olivia's own marriage had spanned sixty years until the death of Uncle Charlie, she considered herself an authority on the subject. She'd lectured them on the importance of being good to one another, of respecting one another and of sharing the responsibility for raising the kids. She'd told them not to make the mistake of taking each other for granted. She also told them that they needed to make time for one another and to listen to what the other one had to say.

"You young people are big on the term *communication.* Well, communication is one of the keys to a good marriage. And that communication needs to start in the bedroom," Aunt Olivia told them. She pointed her cane at him. "You keep your wife happy in the bedroom and the rest will take care of itself."

Lily turned beet-red.

Jack coughed. "Thanks, Aunt Olivia, but I don't think—"

"And you," she said, turning her focus on Lily. "You need to remember that men are like little boys. Every one of them wants to be a super hero between the sheets. If you spend all of your time and energy on the children or the house, you'll be too tired to let them do their super-hero act. Their fragile egos can't handle it. So you make sure you save some of yourself for your man," she continued. "Even if it means ordering takeout food or hiring a sitter for the kids, do it. Because when you close that bedroom door, you need to be a woman first. Understand?"

"Um, yes, ma'am," Lily said, but Jack noted she averted her eyes.

"There's no need for either of you to be embarrassed. From where I stand, it looks to me like you're not having any troubles in the bedroom now. All I'm saying is make sure you keep it that way. Good sex is one of the most important things in a marriage. Why do you think Uncle Charlie and I made it for more than sixty years? It's because we had a good sex life up until the day he died."

Which was a lot more than he wanted to know. "Thanks, Aunt Olivia. We appreciate the advice."

"Yes, thank you," Lily said.

"Just doing my duty," Aunt Olivia told them.

And before she started doling out any more advice on sex, Jack said, "You'll need to excuse us, Aunt Olivia. It looks like Mother needs us to cut the cake." Taking Lily by the arm, he hustled her across the room. "I don't know about you, but I'm ready to get out of this place. What do you say we cut the cake and then head for home?"

"It sounds good to me."

Lily squirmed in the seat of Jack's car. Ever since she'd hit the fourth month of her pregnancy, trips to the restroom were like clockwork. They came at two-hour intervals without fail. She'd gotten used to it for the most part and simply made sure she was in close proximity to a bathroom when the urge hit. But she had been so anxious to leave the reception that she hadn't paid attention to her inner clock or visited the restroom before leaving. As a result, she was well past schedule for a bathroom break and there didn't seem to be a service station anywhere in sight. She shifted in her seat again and wondered what Jack's reaction would be to his new bride ruining the leather upholstery in his shiny Mercedes. She didn't want to find out. "Is it much farther?" she asked him.

"About five minutes," he told her.

Lily bit off a groan and squirmed in her seat.

He glanced across the seat at her. "Is everything okay?" he asked, a worried note in his voice. "Is it the baby?"

"No, everything is not okay, and yes, it's the baby," she confessed and would have laughed at his panicked expression, but knew that even a chuckle right now would result in wet leather seats. "Our little angel is pushing on my bladder and I really, really need a bathroom. So could you please hurry?"

Jack hurried and ten minutes later when she left the bathroom, she felt almost normal again. Or as normal as she could under the circumstances. She had made such a mad dash for the bathroom when they'd arrived that she had scarcely noticed the two-story Colonial and just how lovely it was. After seeing his parents' home, she had worried that Jack, too, lived in a sprawling mansion, and she had wondered how she would feel living in such a big place. But she needn't have worried, because while Jack's house was certainly enormous compared to her efficiency apartment, she didn't find it intimidating.

"I appreciate the offer, Mother…"

Lily heard Jack's deep voice coming from another part of the house and realized he must be on the phone. So she used the time to explore her surroundings. She had raced through the door so quickly, intent on finding the bathroom, that she hadn't noticed that the front door was made of walnut. Nor had she seen the leaded side-lights on either side of the door. Turning, she noted the large rectangular mirror set in pewter that hung over an antique table. A crystal vase of bright red tulips added a burst of color to the muted tones. The sweeping staircase was a real eye-catcher. She walked across the diamond-patterned marble floor and found herself in the living room. The room was gorgeous. A fireplace with a dramatic mantel was the focal point of the room. She could easily imagine a fire burning in the hearth on cold winter days. Floor-to-ceiling windows and built-in bookcases gave the room a welcoming feel. Photographs were scattered about—shots of Jack and his sisters holding skis while they stood in front of a snow-covered slope, shots of his parents on a cruise ship, one of Aunt Olivia standing before a birthday cake covered in candles. She trailed her fingers across the back of one of the couches. The furniture was high-quality and she suspected the chairs alone cost more than all the furniture in her apartment. Yet, it looked comfortable and had a lived-in feel to it. It wasn't just for show.

The living room led to a bright sunroom with flagstone floors, lattice work, ten-foot ceilings and southern, eastern and western exposures. There were French doors leading to a stone patio off the sunroom. Reversing direction, Lily headed back toward the foyer. This time she stopped at the base of the staircase and glanced up to where she suspected the bedrooms were located. Thoughts of the bedrooms and her and Jack's sleeping arrangements set off a nervous fluttering in her stomach.

She hadn't allowed herself to think much beyond the wedding, let alone to the wedding night. She and Jack hadn't discussed what their sleeping arrangements would be. On the one hand, she knew it was silly for them not to share a bed. They were married and it wasn't as though they were two strangers who had never shared a bed. They had. They were expecting a baby together—a baby that had been created the old-fashioned way. But when she'd gone to his room that night, she hadn't realized who he was, that he was Jack Cartwright, a member of Eastwick's elite and the newly appointed board member of Eastwick Cares. No, he had just been the handsome stranger who had eased the ache in her heart. That night, in his arms, it hadn't mattered that she'd failed once again in her quest to discover who she was and why she had been left at the church. What had mattered was that he had wanted her and she had wanted him. And, for that one night, she hadn't felt so alone.

But she had no mask to hide behind now. There was no more pretending she was someone else. She was still Lily. Only now she was pregnant and married to Jack Cartwright, a man who didn't love her, a man who had married her out of his sense of responsibility because she carried his child. She looked at the rings on her finger, remembered the night Jack had given her his grandmother's engagement ring and kissed her. She touched her lips, recalling the rush of heat and emotion she'd experienced that night. She'd felt that same rush of feeling when he'd recited his vows and slid the wedding band on her finger. His voice had sounded so strong and true, she could almost believe that he'd meant those words.

And if you do, Lily Miller, you're setting yourself up for a fall.

It was true, she reasoned. If she had learned nothing else in those years she'd been a ward of the state and in the foster-care system, she had learned not to wear rose-colored glasses. Too many times she had gotten her hopes up, thinking that she would be adopted, only to find herself passed over when the couple she'd pinned her hopes on became pregnant or an infant became available for adoption. Lily Miller would do in a pinch—but only until the real thing came along. Jack might desire her, he might even have married her for the baby's sake. But he didn't love her. The surefire path to heartache would be to allow herself to think otherwise.

"There you are."

She turned at the sound of Jack's voice and darned if her heart didn't kick an extra beat as she watched him walk toward her. He'd lost his jacket, shed his tie and opened the buttons of his shirt at the collar. His dark hair looked a tad less perfect, as though he had shoved his fingers through it. A trace of five o'clock shadow darkened his jawline and made him even sexier than she'd remembered. He looked so tall and strong and sure of himself, she thought. Unlike her, he didn't seem to be suffering any second thoughts or concerns about the fact that they were now husband and wife.

"I'm sorry I left you alone so long. My mother and father arranged for us to have the honeymoon suite at the Embassy

Hotel for the rest of the weekend as a surprise. Apparently the limo driver was supposed to take us there and I screwed things up by dismissing the driver and taking my own car. But I told them we'd take a rain check. I hope that's okay. I thought you might prefer spending some time here, getting used to your new home."

"That's fine and yes, I would. Thank you," she said.

"Have you had a chance to look around yet?"

"Just the living room and the sunroom."

"Do you want me to give you the rest of the tour?"

"I'd like that," she said.

The rest of the house consisted of a formal dining room with a fireplace, paneled walls, mirrored china closets and corner cabinets. The family dining annex had French doors that offered a natural flow out to two great covered porches with ceiling fans. One of the porches had mahogany screens and a fireplace perfect for curling up next to with a book. The country kitchen was custom-made with marble counters, tile floors, glass-fronted cabinets, a teak island for chopping and a six-burner commercial stove. The large bay window looked perfect for a family breakfast table and she could easily see herself, Jack and their baby sitting there.

"The library is this way," Jack said.

The library was cozy. Paneled with old barn siding, it had another great fireplace and coffered ceiling. There was an adjacent bar room with a fridge and ice-maker and a second powder room.

"And this is what I guess you'd call a family room," Jack said as he led her into another large room with a stone fireplace and a coffered ceiling.

Lily moved about the room, took in the details. Built-in bookcases and cabinets completely encircled the room and the cabinets and ceilings were beautifully striated. Oversize chairs, two couches with undertones of forest-green and taupes. It was definitely a man's home. And there lying across the arm of one of the big overstuffed couches was the afghan from her apartment. She walked over to the couch, picked it up and held it to her breast. When she brought her gaze to Jack's again, her voice came out in a hoarse whisper as she asked, "How did this get here?"

"I brought it," he confessed. "While you were getting ready this morning, I went over to your apartment and convinced your building manager to let me inside so I could pick up a few of your things."

"But why?"

"You said you didn't have time this week to see the house or move any of your stuff. I know the rushed wedding, coming here, it's all been hard for you. I thought if you had a few of your things here, it might make you feel more comfortable."

"That was very thoughtful of you. Thank you." His kindness and sensitivity moved her. She was coming to realize that kind, sensitive gestures were not uncommon for Jack. She'd known he was a kind and giving man from his work on the board. He hadn't simply opened his checkbook to help sustain the work they did at Eastwick Cares, he had also given of his time and himself. She'd also seen the way he interacted with his family. Even with his somewhat overbearing aunt Olivia he had shown nothing but patience and caring. She might not have planned this baby, but the better she got to know Jack the more convinced she was that he was going to be a wonderful father to their child. The truth was he would be the perfect husband for her in every way—if only he had married her out of love instead of duty.

"I'll arrange to pick up the rest of your things and your furniture next week and move it in here."

"Somehow, I don't think my furniture will blend very well with your things," she told him, which was the truth. Her furniture was like her—plain, inexpensive, only reproductions of fine antiques. Whereas Jack's furniture was like him—elegant, pricy and genuine antiques passed down through generations.

"We'll make it work," he assured her. "I meant what I said, Lily. I want you to feel comfortable here. This is your home now, too. So if there's anything you don't like about the house, feel free to change it. Or if you decide you don't like the house itself, that you'd rather a live in different architectural style, just say the word and we'll look for another place."

"No. I love the house, Jack. Really. It's warm and welcoming." She looked at him. "It's beautiful just the way it is. I wouldn't change a thing."

"All right. But if you change your mind, just say so. I swear it won't bother me a bit. The important thing to me is that you and the baby are happy here. The vows I took today, I meant them, Lily. I want this marriage to work. I want us to build a life together."

"So do I," she admitted and there was something about the way he looked at her that made her heart beat just a tad faster.

"I know we haven't discussed it much, but I want this to be a real marriage. I want to be a real husband to you and a father to our baby."

"I understand." She did understand, Lily told herself. Jack was a sexy, virile man. He was also an honest one. He wasn't the type of man who would cheat on his wife even if he didn't love that wife.

"I'm glad." He cupped her cheek. "Did you want to rest a while? Or would you like me to show you the upstairs?"

The upstairs was just as impressive as the main floor. There were four bedrooms with baths as well as a sitting room with a fireplace. A huge office with ceiling beams and bamboo trim led to an outdoor terrace. Glass-fronted linen closets and a handy laundry chute lined one section of the hallway. There was another suite with a bath and a private wing that she could have fitted her entire apartment into.

"This leads to the attic," Jack explained, indicating a set of stairs. "We can save viewing it for another time. I'm a little worried about you climbing the narrow steps. But it has two bedrooms, a full bath, a sitting area and a playroom."

"A playroom?"

He grinned. "I'm told the original owners had five children."

Lily swallowed. "Five?"

"Sounds like a lot in this day and age, doesn't it? I imagine it wouldn't be easy to have a family that size. There were just three of us and mealtimes alone were crazy. But as nuts as my family makes me at times, I wouldn't trade any of them. And there's a part of me that thinks it might be nice to have a house filled with kids."

It sounded nice to her, too, Lily admitted silently.

"The master bedroom is down this way," he said and Lily followed him down the hall. He opened the door and motioned for her to enter.

The master bedroom was actually a suite and every bit as lovely as the rest of the house. A stone fireplace took up one wall. A huge mahogany bed took up another. There was a couch and there were more overstuffed chairs. Everything had been done in varying shades of brown, ranging from ivory to mocha. The adjoining bath had his-and-hers sinks, a steam shower and a tub big enough to swim in. There was even some high-tech television built into the mirrored bath wall. Again, it was a room designed for a man.

"This door over here connects to the room next door. I thought you might want to use that room as a nursery. It's close, so we'd be able to hear the baby cry or to handle late-night feedings."

Lily didn't miss the *we* and knew that he expected them to share the room and the big bed. And the truth was, she reminded herself, there was no reason they shouldn't. Yet despite the wedding ring on her finger and the baby growing inside, she couldn't help feeling cheated.

"The dressing rooms and closets are over here. My things are in here," he said and led her into a huge walk-in dressing area and closet. He flipped the light switch and revealed a closet lined with dozens and dozens of suits, shirts, ties and shoes—all neatly arranged on racks and shelves. "I thought you could use this one, but we can swap if you'd like," he offered and opened the door to another dressing room.

She walked over to the vanity table and stared down at her own brush, mirror and the cut-glass perfume bottles that she collected. She picked up the mirror, ran her finger tips along the silver edges. Then she put it down and walked over to the closet. The thing was the size of a small bedroom and there, hanging neatly on the racks and folded on the shelves were the clothes she had packed in the suitcase that morning. She turned and looked at him.

"I had them brought here today while you were getting ready," he explained. "I knew it was going to be a long day and I didn't want you to have to worry about unpacking."

"Thank you. That's was very thoughtful of you."

He nodded and they exited the dressing room. "My mother had the caterers pack up some food for us from the reception. Would you like to rest a bit while I go down and get dinner ready?"

"That sounds good," she said and suddenly realized how tired she was.

"Then you go ahead and relax. I'll let you know when it's time to eat." He kissed her on the forehead and started to leave, only to stop when he reached the end table next to the bed. "I almost forgot. There's one other thing I brought from your apartment, but I wasn't sure where to put him." He pulled open one of the drawers and took out her old battered teddy bear.

"Bentley," she said and took the stuffed animal he held out to her. She clutched him to her. The worn brown bear had been a Christmas gift she'd received from Ellen and Mick Davidson. She had been six and they had been her foster parents for nearly a year by then. They had wanted to adopt her and had begun the paperwork necessary to make her their little girl. She'd been thrilled. At last she was going to have a family, a real mother and father. She had even begun to call them Mom and Dad. Then, in January, Ellen Davidson had discovered she was pregnant with twins. It had been a miracle. After years of trying and failing, they had given up on having a baby. And now they were having two at once. Of course with two babies of their own on the way, they could no longer afford the expense of an adoption. There was also the problem of needing a bigger house that they couldn't afford if they had three children. As much as they loved her, the two little babies needed them more. After they had packed her things and driven her back to the orphanage, Ellen Davidson had been crying. So had she, Lily recalled.

"Please. I promise I'll be good and I won't eat too much or take up too much room," Lily sobbed and clung to the woman she had thought would become her mother.

"You are a good girl," Ellen told her and, taking her by the shoulders, she eased her back. Tears ran down Ellen's cheeks. "You're going to be fine, Lily. And Bentley here is going to keep you company. Aren't you, Bentley? You take care of our Lily until her new parents come, okay?"

Then she handed him to her and Lily clutched the bear to her chest. "What if no one wants me?"

"They will, sweetheart. I promise they will. Before you know it another couple are going to come through that door

take one look at you and scoop you up to take home and be their little girl. Until then, you have Bentley."

Ellen Davidson had been wrong. No one had ever come. No one had ever wanted her to be their little girl.

But she still had Bentley, she thought and felt tears prick her eyes.

"Oh, jeez. Please don't cry," Jack said, stress swimming in his eyes. "I saw him on the bed in your apartment and it looked like you'd had him for a while, so I thought he was special to you. And I thought if I brought him here, it would help you feel more at home. I didn't mean to upset you."

"You didn't upset me," she told him, swallowing back the tears. "Thank you," she said and without thinking, she threw her arms around his waist and hugged him.

For a moment, Jack went stock-still and she was keenly aware of her belly pressing against him, her breasts pressing against his chest. Then his arms slid around her and he held her close. And then something shifted. What was meant to be a hug of gratitude turned into something more.

Lily could feel her pulse speed up. She became much too aware of the hardness of Jack's chest crushed against her breasts, of the flatness of his abdomen against her rounded belly, of the strength of the arms holding her close.

Feeling as though she were treading in dangerous waters, Lily eased away. She looked up at him, saw the heat and the hunger in those deep blue eyes and she saw something more. For no more than a nanosecond, she could have sworn she saw loneliness. And because she'd known what it was to be lonely and alone, she rose up onto her toes and she kissed him.

Seven

In the time since Jack had found Lily again and strongarmed her into marrying him, they had shared all of three kisses. And all three of those kisses had been initiated by him. Not this one, though. This one Lily had initiated all on her own and somehow it all had to do with that rag-tag teddy bear she'd called Bentley.

Bentley, old pal. All I can say is thank you.

Then Lily parted her lips and Jack forgot all about Bentley. He forgot all about the craziness of the past two weeks. He forgot about everything except Lily and how sweet she tasted— liked the almond filling in the wedding cake, like the apple juice in her champagne glass, like innocence and seduction all rolled into one. And he hadn't realized until that moment how very, very much he had been in need of her kiss. He deepened the kiss.

"Jack," she gasped his name and tipped her head back, giving him access to her throat.

He kissed the long slim column, pressed his lips against the pulse point beating in her neck. He heard something hit the carpet, realized it was the bear. Then he couldn't think because Lily was holding on to him, her nails digging into the fabric of his shirt, scoring his shoulders. The sensation was erotic and reminded him of their one night. He had never experienced that type of passion with anyone before. He'd even told himself that making love with her couldn't possibly have been as wonderful as he remembered. He must have been wrong, he realized because being with her now was so much better than he'd remembered. This time he knew the woman in his arms—not just her body, but the woman she was. The woman who clung to a teddy bear from her childhood, the woman who gave of herself and her heart to the teens she worked with, the woman who carried and loved his child, the woman who was now his wife.

His wife.

There had been a time when the idea of taking a wife had sent panic racing through his blood. It was the reason, he figured, he'd managed to dodge the altar for all thirty-three of his years. But he hadn't dodged it today—even when she'd given him every chance to back out. He hadn't taken it. He'd told himself it was because of the baby. He had a responsibility to the baby and to Lily, and he'd never been one to shirk his responsibilities. But he hadn't felt just responsibility and a sense of duty when he'd spoken those vows today. He'd felt…more.

Lily slid her arms around his neck and looked at him. It was the same way she had looked at him that night of the ball—with need and longing and loneliness. And desire. It set off an answering need in him, a need so intense it shocked him. He skimmed his hands down her back, cupped her bottom and pressed her against him. He could feel the swell of her belly and the knowledge that she carried his child made his chest feel full, his heart beat even faster. He wanted to lay

her down on the floor, peel away her gown and make love to
her right there. Instead he slid his arms beneath her knees and
lifted her into his arms. He started toward the bed.

"Jack, what are you doing?" she asked, her voice dazed,
her eyes cloudy.

"I'm going to make love to my wife," he told her and
stopped in front of the bed. Gently he lowered her to the bed.
The first time they'd made love it had been fast and frantic.
He could feel that raw need clawing at him again, the need to
feel her body beneath his, the need to bury himself inside her.
But this time he wanted more than just the heat. He wanted
sweet. He wanted slow. He wanted to savor her, savor them.

Ignoring the hot need rushing through his blood, he took
his time. He started with her hair. Pulling the pins out one by
one, he watched in wonder as the deep red waves tumbled
down around her face and shoulders. He slid his fingers into
all that thick red silk and, holding her head in his hands, he
kissed her. He took his time, savoring each kiss, the shape and
feel of her lips, the sounds of protest she made when he lifted
his head. Never taking his eyes from her face, one by one he
began to unbutton her dress. When he unfastened the last
button, he opened the folds and eased it off her body and
tossed it to the floor. The shapeless ivory satin-and-lace slip
she wore cupped her breasts, sloped along her waist and over
the bump in her middle.

Lily crossed her hands over her breasts.

"I want to see you," he told her. Unlocking her arms, he
placed them on either side of her. She looked like a siren, he
thought, lying with her head on the pillow, her hair a tumble
of copper waves surrounding her face, her lips swollen from
their kisses, her body ripe and womanly. Her breasts were
fuller than he remembered, milk-pale and smooth, spilling
over the lace cups. "You're so beautiful," he told her. H

kissed her shoulder, moved south. He kissed the swell of one
breast, then the other. Then he returned to the first breast and
closed his mouth over the nipple. When he felt the tip harden
beneath the satin, he caught it between his teeth.

Lily gasped, arched her back and it sent desire thundering
through him.

Jack kissed his way down her torso, lingered over the swell
of her belly. Then he moved lower, past her hips, down her
legs. When he reached her ankle, he removed first one ivory
heel, then the other. Then he reversed his journey by kissing
the instep of one stockinged foot before easing his hand up
her leg to kiss her calf, the inside of her kneecap. Pushing the
satin slip higher, he continued his journey.

"Jack," she began and moaned as he pressed a kiss to the
inside of her thigh.

He slid his fingers up to the lacy edge of her stocking. Bless
the person who came up with the lace-topped stockings to
replace panty hose, he thought, as he slipped his fingers inside
the edge of lace. He took his time, easing the stocking down
her leg. When she trembled beneath his touch, his body tightened and he struggled to keep control while he repeated the
process on her other leg. With desire burning in his gut, he
kissed his way back up her torso, along her breasts to her
shoulders, to her mouth. Then he started working his way
down again. When he reached her slender shoulders again, he
began easing down the edge of her slip.

Suddenly Lily went still beneath him. "No," she said and
caught his hand. She scrambled to sit up. "I can't."

Jack froze. "What's wrong?"

She yanked at the coverlet on the bed and clutched it to her
like a shield. "I'm sorry. I shouldn't have…I can't do this."

"Lily, what is it?" He could see the stress swimming in her
eyes, noted her hand on her abdomen. "Is it the baby?" he

asked, panic dousing desire faster than a water hose. "Did I hurt you or the baby?"

"No. No," she said again in a ragged breath. "The baby's fine. And you didn't hurt me."

He sat on the edge of the bed and gulped in air. He felt somewhat relieved—until he saw the expression on Lily's face. She looked horrified. And miserable. And gathered by the way she was hugging herself, she'd rather chew nails than look at him. He started to touch her cheek, but thought better of it. "What's wrong?" When she didn't answer, he said, "Whatever it is, we'll fix it. But you need to tell me what's the matter."

"I…I need some time, Jack."

"I see," he said, and he did. The explosion of chemistry between them hadn't been planned. It had simply happened. It had caught him off-guard, too. While he would have to be a saint to have not wanted to make love with her, he understood her reservations.

"I know we talked about this being a real marriage and a real marriage includes the two of us sleeping together. I mean, it's not like it would be the first time, right?" she said with a self-deprecating laugh that made him hurt for her. "I mean, it's what happened the last time we slept together that got us into this mess in the first place."

"I hardly consider having a beautiful woman become my wife a mess."

"Except that I wouldn't have become your wife if I hadn't gotten pregnant."

It was true, he admitted silently. He wouldn't have gotten married—at least not now—if it hadn't been for the baby. Yet he didn't regret any of it—not the night that led to her pregnancy, not the wedding or the baby on the way. "No one held a gun to my head or yours, Lily. I have no regrets about marrying you or the baby."

"You're a good man, Jack Cartwright. And a kind one," she told him. "And I'm grateful for everything—the trusts you set up for me and the baby, for not making me feel immoral and irresponsible for getting us both in this fix in the first place."

"I seem to recall I had a hand in that," he told her, hoping to ease her anxiety.

"But a lot of men wouldn't have felt that way. Most men in your position wouldn't have accepted the responsibility and if they did, they wouldn't have offered marriage."

"I'm not most men, Lily. What I am is your husband and I want to be a real husband to you in every way."

"I know," she said as she knotted her fingers in the coverlet. "And it's what we agreed to."

"But it's too soon for you," Jack said, unable to bear seeing Lily torture herself further.

"Yes," she said and there was such relief in her voice that Jack didn't know whether to be insulted or hug her. "You have every reason to be angry, Jack. I never should have let things go so far just now."

"I'm not angry. Just disappointed."

"I'm sorry," she told him.

"You don't need to be sorry. I'm as much to blame as you are for what almost happened just now. Probably more so. I want you, Lily. I have from the first time I set eyes on you at that ball. Nothing that's happened during the months in between or in these past two weeks has changed that. You needing time to get used to the idea of me being your husband won't change it either. I still want you, but I can wait until you're ready."

"Thank you. For being so understanding."

He nodded. "I want this marriage to work, Lily. I intend for this marriage to work," he amended. If the business world had taught him nothing else, it had taught him that he was the one in control of his destiny. He was the one who was responsible for whether he succeeded or failed. He didn't intend for his marriage to fail. But right now Lily needed time and he needed patience. He stood. "Are you hungry?"

"A little," she admitted.

"Then why don't you freshen up while I go downstairs and see what I can put together for our dinner?"

"That sounds good."

And as Jack left the room and headed downstairs, he couldn't help thinking that this was turning out to be one hell of a wedding night.

Lily sat up in bed with a start. She looked around the room at the strange surroundings and for a moment she forgot where she was. Then the moonlight spilling in through the windows caught the ring on her finger. She stared down at the diamond ring and wedding band on her left hand. And it all came rushing back—the wedding at Jack's parents' home, the drive out to his house, the two of them almost making love. She could feel her cheeks heat as she remembered allowing him to undress her, to touch her and then pulling back. It had been unfair of her to do that to him, she admitted. Just as it had been unfair of her to accept his offer that she take the room and he move to the spare bedroom next door.

She attempted to pull her knees up to her chest to hug them, but had to settle for resting her hands atop her belly. Heavens, what a mess, she thought. By all rights, Jack should have been furious with her. Regardless of the reasons for their marriage, they were man and wife. And he had never pulled any punches with her about their marriage, including sex. She knew from experience that there was nothing wrong with Jack's libido. Nor hers apparently, she thought, still somewhat embarrassed by her actions. Yet as much as she had wanted him, she admitted, she hadn't been able to follow through. Some voice deep inside her had caused her to pull back, reminding her about Sister Dorothy's lecture when she had had her first serious crush and found herself pressured to have sex.

"Remember, Lily. Sex without love is like tossing a lit match into the sea," the nun told her. *"It dies out in an instant and all you're left with is the cold, empty sea."*

It was crazy, Lily told herself. Worse, it was foolish. Jack Cartwright was handsome, wealthy and sexy as sin. He was also a good man, an honest man who was kind and gentle, a man you could count on. He was a man who was sensitive enough to recognize that an old battered teddy bear was more to her than just stuffing. Reaching for Bentley, she held him close and buried her face in him.

She could all too easily fall in love with the man. In fact, it wouldn't take much for her to do just that—especially when he looked at her. Jack had a way of looking at her as if she were the only woman in the world. And when he held her in his arms, he made all the years of disappointment melt away. In his arms, she felt like she was…like she was home. He had made her feel that same way the night of the ball. That night she had felt so alone and unwanted. Then he had come to her, taken her in his arms and during those hours she'd spent in his room, he had made her feel less alone. He had made her feel loved.

And how had she repaid him? By asking him to spend his wedding night alone in the next room. Some way to start off her marriage, she thought, guilt nagging at her. Jack deserved so much better. He deserved so much more. He deserved to be married to a woman he loved. That woman wasn't her.

The baby chose that moment to kick a fifty-yard field goal—or at least that's what it felt like, Lily thought. The little angel also was having a good old time pushing on her bladder and reminding her it had been a good three hours since she'd been for a potty visit. Laying Bentley aside, she pulled off the covers and headed for the bathroom.

By the time she'd washed her hands and returned to the bedroom, she was wide awake. And she was hungry. A glance at the clock told her it was not yet four in the morning. But she knew from experience there would be no going back to sleep for her. She'd concluded some time ago that her baby was a night person, since it seemed to be most restless between the hours of midnight and dawn. Of course that meant she spent a great deal of her day feeling tired and wishing for a nap.

Fortunately, her workload had begun to decrease, as it always did at this time of year. She reached for her robe and slipped it on over the peach-colored gown. Evidently the school system—or perhaps it was the number crunchers who employed the school counselors—figured troubled teens didn't need guidance during the summer months, because most of the students discontinued their sessions. Those who did come were usually referred from state agencies. It concerned her, she admitted as she belted her robe and dug under the bed for her slippers. That's why she'd always tried to make herself available for any of the kids who needed her. But with her pregnancy progressing, she was glad she had been able to get a graduate student in family counseling as a volunteer to help fill in for her.

After pushing her feet into her fuzzy slippers, she gently closed the bedroom door and gave herself a moment to get her bearings. Pleased to see the night-light in the hall, she padded down the carpeted hallway and practically held her breath as she passed Jack's door. The last thing she wanted to do was to wake him up so early, she reasoned. He'd been so sweet and wonderful to her over dinner. He hadn't pressured her or even commented again on the halt she'd called to their lovemaking. Instead he had gone out of his way to make her relax, telling her silly stories about his mother's cooking fiascoes and making her laugh at his tales of growing up with two annoying younger sisters. Never once had he mentioned what had to have been on his mind—that this was his wedding night and instead of doing what most grooms did with their brides, he was sitting in the kitchen serving her milk in a champagne glass and feeding her leftover wedding cake for dessert. And the more understanding and patient Jack had been, the more miserable she had felt. It was the reason she had cried herself to sleep. Or at least that's what she'd told herself because she didn't want to think, not even for a second, that her tears had anything to do with the fact that she had married a man who didn't love her.

She made her way down the grand staircase and when she reached the bottom, she was struck once again by the beauty of the house. And it was a big house, she reminded herself as she tried to remember in which direction was the kitchen. After only one wrong turn, she found it. She flipped on the light switch. The room was a cook's dream, she thought, noting the sub-zero refrigerator, the six-burner stove and grill, the convection oven and chopping block. She walked across the tiled floor to the refrigerator and opened the door. The thing was packed. In addition to the shelf filled with containers of leftover food from the reception, there were three kinds of juice, milk, fresh vegetables, eggs, cheeses, cold cuts and tons more. It didn't take much in the way of deduction to realize that Jack had stocked the place with food in anticipation of her moving in. One more thoughtful thing he had done with her in mind.

Not sure whether she wanted to whip up an early breakfast for herself or indulge in a very-late-night snack, she pulled open the freezer. And she could have kissed Jack when she saw the two gallons of butter pecan ice cream. A late-night snack it was, she decided as she pulled out the container of ice cream and made her way to the table.

But one-third of the way through the bowl of ice cream, she was struck with a major craving for eggs. An omelet to be precise—one with tomatoes and cheese and ham and some of the peppers and onions she'd seen in the fridge. She gathered all the ingredients, put them on the counter by the stove and checked out the cabinets in search of a skillet. She found it and went to work.

Fifteen minutes later, she had the fixings simmering in butter in the skillet. She whipped some milk and a spoonful of mayonnaise with the eggs and added them to the skillet. When it was ready, she folded the omelet over. Turning off the burner, she put the cover on the skillet and set it aside. There was only one thing she needed to complete her omelet feast—some tuna fish and peanut butter on the side. She found the peanut butter and was scouring the pantry for a can of tuna. She spied it on an upper shelf and was just reaching for it when a hand reached over her and scooped it from the shelf.

"Here you go."

Lily took the can with the white-and-green label and slowly turned around. Her stomach fluttered as she looked at Jack. He hadn't bothered with a shirt or shoes. He wore only jeans slung low at the waist with the top button un- done. His chest looked strong, his shoulders incredibly broad and there were just enough muscles to inform her that Jack didn't spend all of his time behind a desk or arguing in a courtroom. His hair was mussed. A dark shadow cov- ered his jaw reminding her of that TV hunk Patrick Demp- sey who played a doctor on some prime-time show. But it was his eyes, those smoky blue eyes, staring at her that made her feel like a clumsy school girl. She dropped the can of tuna.

Jack yelped and grabbed his toe.

"Oh my God, I'm sorry," she said and followed him out of the pantry.

"It's all right," he told her as he limped over to the table and sat. He grabbed his big toe in his hand.

"Are you sure? Maybe I should take a look at it. You could have broken the skin."

"It's okay," he insisted, but he continued to clutch his foot.

"How do you know? You haven't even looked at it," she pointed out and knelt down to examine his foot. "Now quit being a big baby and let me see."

Finally he released his foot long enough to allow her to have a peek at it. There was a big red welt on his toe and she suspected he was going to have a nasty bruise. She looked up at him. "I don't think you'll be kicking a soccer ball around for a few days, but other than some bruising, I think you'll live."

"Thank you, Dr. Cartwright."

She grinned. "You're welcome. I'll get you some ice to put on it to keep the swelling down," she said and as gracefully as she could considering she had a mini-watermelon for a belly, she stood.

"You don't have to do that," he told her and reached out to help her stand.

The contact had her belly brushing against him and she was much too much aware of the dark hair on his naked chest arrowing down toward his jeans. She stepped back and tried to shake off the sexual images running through her head. "Sit down," she said.

"But, Lily—"

"Sit," she told him again and pointed to the chair. Once he had done as she instructed, she said, "Getting you some ice is the least I can do, considering I'm the one who put that toe out of commission in the first place."

"I didn't realize I married such a bossy woman."

She smiled. "It's too late for you to change your mind now," she teased. "You're stuck with me. Your mother already ordered us engraved thank-you cards."

"Trust me, I haven't changed my mind."

The seriousness of his tone and the darkening of his eyes had her pulse jumping again. "Plastic bags?" she asked, unwilling to travel down that road again.

"Second drawer on the left."

After retrieving one of the zippered bags, she filled it with ice, wrapped it in a dishtowel and then brought it back over to Jack. "Let's see the toe, big guy."

"I do own an ice bag, you know," he advised her as he unclenched the fist holding the toe.

"Seeing as how you have every gadget known to mankind, I was pretty sure that you did. But this works just fine for me," she told him and applied the makeshift ice bag to the reddened toe. Holding the cold pack to his foot, she looked up at him. "Since I doubt that you're usually up at this hour of the morning, I'm going to guess that I'm the reason you're down here. I'm sorry I woke you, I didn't realize I was making so much racket."

"You weren't. The acoustics in here are state-of-the art. You could bang the pots on the wall and I wouldn't hear it upstairs. The truth is, I didn't even know you were in here until I saw the lights on."

She narrowed her eyes. "Since you never mentioned anything about being a sleepwalker, what were you doing down here at this time of the morning?"

"Would you believe I was looking for a midnight snack?" He glanced over at the stove and sniffed. "Is that onion I smell?"

"No, I don't believe you were looking for a midnight snack because midnight was about four and a half hours ago. And yes, those are onions you smell. And ham and bell peppers and a half dozen other things. I made an omelet."

She lifted the ice pack, looked at the toe and was pleased to see that it wasn't as swollen. "So why *are* you down here?"

"I wanted to check on you."

Puzzled, she asked, "Why would you need to check on me?"

"Well, you were up a little past ten and again around one to go to the bathroom. Then after you made your trip at four, you came downstairs. When you didn't come back up, I got worried and thought I'd better make sure you were okay."

Lily felt her face redden. "I didn't realize I made so much noise."

"You didn't. I'm just a light sleeper and I...well, I was worried about you. I've been reading up on stuff about pregnancy. Do you have any idea how many women go into labor early? A lot," he told her before she could answer. "And one of the main reasons is stress and let's face it, I haven't made your life exactly stress-free lately. If anything happened to you or the baby, I couldn't live with myself."

Oh, Lord, Lily thought. But the man was making it awfully hard for her not to love him. "Nothing's going to happen to me or the baby," she promised him.

He eyed her solemnly. "I'm going to hold you to that." Then as though he sensed her emotions were running high, he sniffed the air and said, "That omelet sure smells good."

She grinned, happy that the moment was over. "Would you like some?"

"Only if you have enough."

"We'll make it enough," she told him. She got out two plates, served them both and poured them each a glass of milk. Then she retrieved the can of tuna and opened it.

"What's that for?" he asked.

She dished out the tuna and carried it to the table, along with the jar of peanut butter. "It's to go with my omelet." She heaped tuna and peanut butter on her plate, mixed them together and arranged a forkful of the odd mixture with a bite of omelet. "Want to try it?"

"No, thanks," he told her and she nearly laughed at his horrified expression. "This is a pregnancy thing, right? Just a crazy craving? I mean this isn't a regular deal, is it?"

She laughed. "I've only discovered the combination since I've been pregnant. But it's one of my favorites."

"There are others?" he asked warily.

"A few. But I guess my favorite is potato-chip-and-banana sandwiches."

"Potato-chip-and-banana sandwiches," he repeated. "I can handle that," he assured her and with a gusto every cook appreciated, he dug into the omelet.

When they'd finished eating and set the kitchen to rights, Lily was stuffed, relaxed and enjoying Jack's company. She knew he had gone out of his way to put her at ease, just as he had earlier at dinner by telling her tales about his family and some of his embarrassing moments as a young man. It had been hard to imagine the formidable Jack Cartwright as anything but perfect. So listening to him made her appreciate him even more.

When she yawned for the third time, Jack stood and said, "Now that I've bored you to tears, do you think you can get back to sleep?"

"You didn't bore me," she assured him and yawned again.

He laughed. "Right." He led her from the kitchen, turned out the light.

"It's true. It's our little angel here that's the problem," she explained. "Our baby is a night owl and thinks Mommy should be one, too. Of course, the darling doesn't understand that I have to get up in the morning and there are no nap times for grownups."

"You can sleep in this morning. And in case you haven't heard, I'm a very rich man. So you really don't have to work."

"I want to," she told him as they climbed the stairs together. She'd made that decision right at the start. The last thing she wanted to do was to allow herself to become dependent on Jack. Situations changed, people changed. She'd learned quickly in the foster-care system that she should never count on anything or anyone but herself. While Jack might have good intentions, sometimes those good intentions changed, too. They had with the Davidsons.

Jack walked her to her bedroom door, opened it for her. "I enjoyed tonight."

"Me, too."

"Goodnight, Mrs. Cartwright," he told her and lowering his head he kissed her. The kiss was sweet, tender and over much too soon. "I'll see you in the morning. And I'll fix breakfast."

Jack fixed breakfast that morning and the next three mornings as well. A routine developed where he cooked breakfast, they both pitched in for the evening meal and the midnight snacks were under her direction. The best part of the day though came with the goodnight kiss at her bedroom door. Those kisses had grown deeper, longer and more passionate by the day, she admitted. She'd reached the point where she looked forward to them. The way she had looked forward to this one, she thought as she wrapped her arms around him and gave herself to the kiss.

Her breasts had grown more sensitive during her pregnancy. Beneath the thin robe, she could feel her nipples tighten as they pressed against his chest, sending that sizzle through her blood again. He cupped her bottom, pulling her closer, and the sensation of his arousal against her belly left her weak with desire. When he lifted his head, she was tempted to draw his mouth back down to hers.

"I'd better let you get some sleep," he told her in a voice husky with desire. "And I'd better go take a cold shower."

"Jack," she called out when he reached the door of his room. "Yes?"

"Nothing. I just wanted to say goodnight and that I'll see you at breakfast."

The disappointment in his eyes was clear. "Right. See you at breakfast," he said and disappeared inside his room.

What was she waiting for? Lily asked herself as she climbed into her bed and reached for Bentley. The man was caring and considerate, honest and straightforward. How many men would get up all during the night just to be sure that the pregnant wife who won't sleep with them got up to go to the bathroom? Probably none. Except Jack Cartwright. The truth was that Jack was flat-out wonderful. Everything about marriage to Jack Cartwright was wonderful.

And it scared her to bits.

She was falling in love with him, Lily admitted as she hugged Bentley and snuggled under the covers. Maybe she had loved Jack all along and had simply refused to accept it. Either way, the realization of just how important Jack had become to her terrified her. She'd been this close before to believing she belonged—with the Davidsons, all those times when she'd gotten a new clue that she thought would lead her to her mother. And each time, she'd had the rug yanked out from under her. Each time she had been left alone and lonelier than before.

Suppose he met someone? Suppose he fell in love with someone and realized what a mistake he'd made by marrying her? Suppose he wanted a divorce? It certainly was possible.

No, more like probable, she amended and was crushed by how much just thinking of that possibility hurt.

She was being ridiculous, Lily told herself and punched at her pillow. Jack had made sure that both she and the baby would be taken care of financially. He might not love her, but he did love his child. And he wanted her. Somehow, she would have to find a way to make his desire for her be enough.

And what happens when the desire burns out?

She would go on just as she had gone on all the times before when she'd found herself alone. Only this time, she wouldn't be alone. She would have her baby—Jack's baby. Placing a protective hand on her stomach, Lily drifted off to sleep and she dreamed…

Lily ran. The hospital corridor was dark. Too dark. And it was cold. Why was the hospital so cold and empty? she wondered. She ran to the nurses' station, but no one was there. Where was everyone? And where were Jack and her baby? She spied the sign indicating the nursery and ran toward it. That's where her baby was. Her beautiful little girl with her red hair and Jack's blue eyes was in the nursery. Wasn't that what the nurse had said?

"We need to take her to get cleaned up, Mrs. Cartwright. We'll bring her back in a few minutes," the nurse had promised as she took the baby from her arms and disappeared out of the room.

"Jack, where are you going?" she asked when he started to leave.

"I'm going to call my parents. You just rest and I'll be back."

But he hadn't come back. Not that day nor the next. And they hadn't brought her baby back either. Frantic, she ran to the nursery and searched the babies in the window, looking for her little girl. But she wasn't there. There was no Baby Girl

Cartwright. Panic pumped through her blood. "Nurse," she said, grabbing hold of the woman passing her. "Baby Girl Cartwright, she isn't in the nursery. Where is she?"

The woman looked at her clipboard. "Oh, she's gone. Her father took her home."

Lily screamed.

Eight

"Lily. Lily, wake up," Jack pleaded as he sat on the edge of the bed and caught Lily by the shoulders. He'd aged ten years when he'd heard the blood-curdling scream coming from the bedroom and he had never been so terrified in his life.

He still was.

Though she had stopped screaming, chalk had more color than she did. Her blue eyes were the size of quarters and filled with terror. And she was trembling so badly, he could have sworn he heard her teeth chatter. He hauled her into his arms and she clung to him. He kissed her head, stroked her back. "It's all right. It was just a bad dream. I'm here," he whispered, repeating the mantra over and over until the shaking subsided. Jack wasn't sure how long he sat there holding her. It could have been five minutes. It might have been an hour. From the position of the moon in the sky, he suspected that dawn was still hours away.

Finally, she loosened her grip on him and eased back a fraction. "Thank you," she said, her voice barely audible.

"Nothing to thank me for. I'm your husband." She had a little more color in her cheeks now and while she no longer looked terrified there was a loneliness there that had a fist tightening around his heart. "Do you want to talk about it?"

"Not yet. I need to go to the bathroom."

When she returned a few minutes later and crawled back into bed, she seemed to be over the worst of whatever nightmare had plagued her. "It's going to be morning soon and you need your rest. Would you like me to get you some warm milk to help you sleep?"

She shook her head.

"How about some ice cream? I think I saw another carton of butter pecan in the freezer," he said, hoping to somehow ease her by teasing.

"No. No ice cream. I'm okay now."

But she didn't look okay. She looked lost and alone and sad. Not just sad but that reach-inside-and-rip-out-your-heart kind of sad. It was that sadness that made his own heart feel heavy and helpless because he didn't know what to do for her. In the days since their wedding, they had spent time together getting to know one another. They had shared meals, domestic duties and kisses so steamy that they would have made a monk turn to sin. But she had continued to keep him at arms' length. He'd exercised a patience he hadn't known he'd possessed when he left her at the bedroom door each night. He'd developed an abhorrence for cold showers, but he'd promised himself and her that they would not share a bed until she was ready. She gave no indication she wanted him to stay now— not even to comfort her.

Reluctant to leave her, but unsure what to do, he said, "I guess I'd better let you try to get back to sleep then." He stood, picked up Bentley from the floor and tucked the bear in bed beside her. Leaning over, he kissed her gently on the lips. "I'll leave the door open. Just call if you need me."

"Jack," she said and he turned. "Don't go. I want you to stay."

She didn't have to ask him twice. He went to her, slid into the bed beside her and took her in his arms. He held her. It felt good to hold her like this, he thought and was content to just be close to her. If anyone had bet him a month ago that he could spend what seemed like hours holding a woman who he'd wanted to make love to in his arms and not become frustrated, he'd have taken the bet.

And he would have lost.

Lying in bed with his arms wrapped around Lily, he couldn't help thinking how good it felt to hold her this way. Not only did it feel good, it felt right. The one night they'd spent together, neither of them had spent much time just cuddling. He'd wanted her too much and she had wanted him. The lovemaking had been explosive, leaving little energy or inclination for anything more. There was so much more, he realized.

Jack wasn't sure how long he lay there just holding Lily. Long enough for the tremors to stop. Long enough for her breathing to settle. She remained silent and he didn't press her to tell him about the dream that had terrified her. He simply waited and trusted that she would talk when she was ready.

When Lily finally did begin to talk, she didn't tell him about the dream. Instead she told him about growing up in the orphanage and foster homes, about hoping that her mother would someday come back for her or some couple would make her their own. She told him about being alone.

"On that night of the ball, I'd been wired for days. The detective I'd hired had a lead on my locket. It's not a common design and the detective had finally tracked down the jeweler who'd made it. The jeweler was a master artisan and was sure if he saw the piece, he could tell us who purchased it," she began. "I was so sure that I'd find out who purchased the locket and that person would lead me to my mother. I even allowed myself to imagine what it would be like meeting her, what we would say to each other."

"What happened?"

"It turned out that the jeweler had Alzheimer's and while he did have good days where his mind was sharp, most of the time he had trouble remembering his own wife."

Jack ached for her. She'd mentioned briefly about the locket being her only legacy. Even knowing the circumstances of her upbringing he still hadn't been able to imagine just how deep her pain and loneliness had been. How deep they still were.

"It wasn't the first time I'd hit a brick wall in my search to find out who I was. You get used to disappointments and usually I can handle them. But that night, I couldn't. When I arrived at the ball, I'd never felt so alone in my life. And then you were there, asking me to dance," she explained. "And the moment you took me into your arms, all the loneliness and disappointment seemed to melt away. All I could see, all I could think of was you."

He understood, because he had reacted in much the same way to her. Desire for a woman had never been so sharp, passion never so intense for him as it was that night with Lily. He'd broken a string of his own rules that night. Yet he had never regretted it. He still didn't. "If that's what the bad dream was about, that you feel you made a mistake that night, I understand. But—"

"No. That's not what I'm saying. I just wanted you to know why I did what I did that night." She turned over, looked into his eyes. She brought her hand to his face. "I don't regret making love with you that night, Jack. It was wonderful. *You* were wonderful. I wouldn't change that night for anything even if I could."

"Neither would I," he told her and turned his mouth into her palm and kissed it.

"This baby growing inside me, it means everything to me. Everything. It's…it's my family. For the first time in my life I really will have a family."

"You have a family now, Lily. You have me. You have my parents, my sisters, all of my relatives. They're your relatives, too," he assured her. "Is that what the dream was about? You dreamed about being alone?"

She told him about the dream. About waking up and finding him gone, their baby gone, once again being left with no one.

"Lily, sweetheart, it was just a bad dream. A nightmare. I promise you, you have nothing to worry about. I'm not going anywhere and I would never take our baby from you."

"You could meet someone…someone you love and want to be with."

"So could you," he pointed out and he was surprised at the flash of anger that came with that notion. "If you're worried I'll be unfaithful to you, don't. You're my wife and I meant those vows we took."

"But—"

"No buts. And no more bad dreams. We're a family now, Lily. You and me and our baby, we're a family." He pressed a kiss to her lips. "It'll be morning soon. You should try to get some sleep."

For once she didn't argue with him. He wrapped his arms around her, held her close and she seemed to rest. When the baby kicked and she stirred, he moved his hand to her belly and that seemed to put her at ease. After a while, he realized she was asleep.

Unfortunately, sleep didn't come nearly as easily for him.

Her scent surrounded him. She was soft, incredibly soft, and each time she moved, brushed against him, it was heaven and it was hell. Sighing, Jack settled his arm around her and resigned himself to the fact that it was going to be a very long night.

Lily felt surrounded by warmth. It was a wonderful feeling, like being wrapped in a blanket in front of a fire while a blizzard raged outside. Content, she burrowed into that warmth and hugged the arm that was around her waist. *The arm around her waist?* Lily opened her eyes. She glanced down and sure enough, there was a strong arm dusted with dark hair anchored just below her breasts.

Suddenly the events of the previous night came rushing back—the nightmare, Jack coming into her room and holding her, her asking him to stay, lying in the dark and telling him about the dream. It didn't take a shrink to tell her why she'd had that dream.

She could blame it on stress. She could blame it on hormones or on the fact that she'd had her life turned upside-down. It was probably a combination of all those things. It was also because she had been scared—scared of her feelings for Jack. And it was those feelings that were the problem, she admitted. When they had agreed to marry, he had been straightforward. So had she. They were marrying to provide a two-parent home for their baby. As two healthy, sexually compatible adults, sex was expected to be a part of the marriage. Love wasn't. Love didn't even factor into the equation. She had agreed to it all. Only she'd changed the rules in the middle of the game. She'd fallen in love with her husband.

What was that old adage about the best-laid plans? She'd thought she was so smart, keeping Jack at an emotional distance even though they were man and wife. She had considered herself a pro at knowing where to draw that line. After all, she'd done it most of her life. It had been the first rule of survival that she'd learned in the foster-care system—to share only a part of herself and to always, always guard her heart. If she didn't give her heart, she would never run the risk of having it broken. But the strategy hadn't worked. Somewhere between the crazy midnight forays in the kitchen and him holding her after a bad dream, she had fallen in love with the man.

Now what, Lily girl? You're in love with your husband, but he doesn't love you.

It was true, she admitted. Jack didn't love her, that was a given. But he did care about her. He had to care about her because no man would put up with her crazy cravings or disrupt his own sleep just to be sure she was okay after going to the bathroom. No man could kiss her the way he kissed her or treat her with such patience and tenderness if he didn't at least care about her. And he wanted her. Jack cared about her and desired her. Would that be enough?

She would make it enough, Lily told herself.

She could feel Jack lying next to her, his chest against her back and there was no mistaking the hard ridge pressed against her. She stroked the arm around her middle with her fingers.

"You're awake."

Slowly Lily turned around and looked into his eyes—those deep blue eyes that could be so cool and so warm at the same time. "Yes, I'm awake."

"Feeling better?" he asked.

"Yes. Thanks for staying with me last night."

He kissed her lightly on the lips, then ran the back of his fingers gently along the curve of her face. "Any time. It's almost time for us to get up and get ready for work. So what do you say to me making some French toast this morning?"

"I don't want French toast," she told him.

"All right. What about a western omelet?"

She shook her head and before he could offer her another choice of breakfast entree, Lily kissed him. She kissed him long and slow, trying to tell him in that kiss how much she loved him, how much she wanted him. When she finished with his mouth, she pushed up to her knees and went to work on his neck, his shoulder. She kissed his chest, ran her tongue around his nipple and continued down the dark V of hair arrowing to his belly. When she reached his pajama bottom and unsnapped the first button, Jack caught her hand.

For a moment Lily froze. She thought she'd made a mistake. Maybe he didn't want her. She couldn't blame him. Her hair was a mess. Her eyes were probably still puffy from crying and she looked as though she had swallowed a soccer ball. Not exactly a combination for seduction.

Then he said, "I want you, Lily. So much that I can hardly see straight. But you're vulnerable right now. You don't have to do this just because I was here for you last night."

Able to breathe again, she said, "This has nothing to do with last night. It's because I want you, too." After ridding Jack of his pajama bottoms and briefs, Lily set about reacquainting herself with his body. He was magnificent—long, toned limbs, firm muscles and abs. Emboldened by the evidence of his arousal, she smoothed her hands over him and followed where her fingers had been with her mouth.

She wished she were a sculptress so she could capture him in clay. Then she wished she were an artist so that she could capture his face on canvas. It was such a wonderful face. Strong jaw, slashing cheekbones, a nose that looked as if it might have suffered a break sometime in the past, steel-blue eyes that could be as cool as a Connecticut winter or as hot as a tropical sun. And his mouth—a generous, no-nonsense mouth that she knew from personal experience was capable of magical things.

"Lily," he whispered and hauled her up so that he could kiss her with that mouth. But he didn't stop with her mouth. He kissed her eyes, her jaw, nipped at her ear and made his way to her throat. He pulled the gown over her head, tossed it to the floor. Then he resumed his assault on her senses, moving from her shoulders to her breast. He drew a circle around her nipple with his tongue and when he took the tip into his mouth, Lily sucked in her breath.

"Jack," she called out, not sure for what she was asking him.

Yet he seemed to know because he continued to make love to her with his mouth, that clever, oh, so clever mouth that seemed to know just where each sensitive spot was. He eased her down on to the bed and started all over again. "You don't know how badly I've wanted to do this," he told her as he worked his way down her body.

She had a fairly good idea, Lily wanted to tell him, but then she could barely think, let alone speak when he lingered at her belly, paying particular attention to the swollen mound.

"You are so beautiful," he whispered and tugged her panties down.

She knew she looked like a soccer ball on stilts, but Jack made her feel beautiful. And then she couldn't think at all because he was opening her to him, tasting her. Lily shivered at the sensations rolling through her. She gripped the sheets with her fists, unable to speak, barely able to breathe. When she thought she could stand the pleasure no longer, he replaced his mouth with his fingers. He brought her up again, sent her crashing over with the waves again and again. Then he was inside her, one long, slow, deep stroke and another and another, each one pulling at her heart. How she loved him, she thought, wishing that she dare tell him, but afraid to say the words aloud.

"Don't hold back, Lily," he urged.

She didn't. The waves came crashing over her once more, like the rush of the ocean against the shore. But still he resisted. "I won't break, Jack," she assured him when she saw that he was holding back.

"I know," he managed. "But I don't want to hurt you or the baby."

"You won't," she assured him, and then she proceeded to prove it by pushing him down onto his back and straddling him. She began to move, following the same slow rhythm he had set. The sensations were exquisite, the look in his eyes empowering as he gripped her hips and helped her move. His eyes never left her face as she moved up and down, up and down. And then, like a storm brewing, she could feel the pressure building again, growing tighter and tighter until she felt herself explode.

"Jack," she cried. Then she blurted out, "I love you." She wasn't sure if he heard her, then it didn't matter because the world was splintering into bright lights and he was shouting her name.

Later when she lay in his arms, Lily told herself that this would be enough. She would make it enough. She had to.

"The contracts for the new Falcon venture are in the folder for you to look over," Jack's assistant Claire told him as he sat at his desk reviewing the morning's schedule. She continued to run through a list of ongoing cases, trial dates and phone messages. But his thoughts drifted to Lily.

Ever since that night last week when they'd made love for the first time as man and wife, things had changed between them. Lily was more at ease with him and she seemed happy. He was happy, too, Jack admitted. It was as if all those uncertainties that had been like a wall between them had dissipated. He found himself anxious to get home in the evenings and reluctant to leave in the mornings. It wasn't just the lovemaking, although that was beyond terrific. It was being with Lily, sharing things with her, like her crazy food cravings. It was learning all those little things a husband and wife knew about each other. Like the way he now knew that Lily loved old musicals and laughed out loud at the Peanuts comic strips. Like the way her eyes lit up at the sight of a kitten and how she loved a ragged teddy bear named Bentley. Like the way she shivered when he kissed that sensitive spot on her spine.

Face it, Cartwright. You're a happily married man.

When the room fell silent, Jack realized that he'd missed something and that Claire was waiting for an answer. "I'm sorry, what was that?"

"I said Mr. Carlton called. He wants to know if you can meet him for drinks on Monday."

Jack hesitated. He hadn't spoken to Carlton since before his wedding. The political power broker had been as stunned as everyone else when Jack had announced he was getting married. He had also explained his decision not to run for the senate seat. He had known that Carlton was disappointed, but Jack had felt he'd made the right decision. With a new wife and a baby on the way, he honestly didn't want to divert any of his time or attention to working a campaign. But perhaps he owed it to Carlton to hear him out and explain his decision process in person. "Tell him okay and see if he can meet me at the country club." He made himself a notation. "Okay, what else have we got?"

"You have a ten-thirty with Alexandra Gifford and you're due in court this afternoon at two o'clock."

"Thanks, Claire," Jack told his assistant, who nodded and started to leave the office. "Claire?"

"Yes, sir?"

"Call Dr. Emily Robinson," he instructed, referring to the obstetrician whose care Lily was under. "My wife has an ap-

pointment with her today for a checkup. Find out what time
it's for."

"Yes, sir."

Although Lily had told him it wasn't necessary for him to
accompany her to the appointment, he wanted to be there
with her. This was a special time for both of them and while
he may have not been there for her the first five months, he
intended to be with her for the last four—and all the months
and years that followed. When the intercom buzzed, he said,
"Yes, Claire?"

"Mrs. Cartwright's appointment is for eleven o'clock, sir."

Eleven o'clock. Jack looked at his calendar. "Claire, see if
you can reschedule Alexandra Gifford for late this afternoon
or tomorrow morning."

"Yes, sir."

Jack pushed back from his chair, walked across the room
to retrieve his suit coat from the closet and left his office. "I'll
be back after lunch," he told his assistant. "If you need to reach
me, I have a stop to make and then I'll be at Dr. Robinson's
with my wife."

"Yes, sir," Claire said, but Jack didn't miss the grin.

"Something funny?"

"No, sir. I was just thinking how lucky Mrs. Cartwright is."

"I'm the one who's lucky," he told her. And he was, Jack
thought as he left the office and headed for the parking lot.
Yes, he was one very lucky man.

It was because he felt so lucky that thirty minutes later he
was leaving the jewelry store on Main Street with one of the
shop's signature bags. When he reached his car, he slid inside
and placed the jeweler's bag next to the one from the toy store.
A check of his watch told him he had fifteen minutes, so he
headed to Dr. Robinson's office.

He made it to the doctor's office in twelve minutes flat, and when he walked in the door, he found Lily sitting in the waiting area, her nose buried in a parenting magazine. Dressed in a soft pink top and white slacks with her hair pulled up on top of her head, she looked far younger than twenty-seven. And, were it not for the definitive bump in her belly, he wouldn't have known she was pregnant. Even well into her fifth month of pregnancy, her legs and hips had remained slim. Her breasts were fuller, but not overly large and even while reading a magazine, she held herself with the grace of a ballerina. Her cream-colored skin literally glowed. Even the faint dusting of freckles across her nose had a glow about them.

As though she'd sensed him watching her, Lily looked up from the magazine. Her eyes widened in surprise. "Jack, what are you doing here?"

"Meeting my wife." He shut the door, and, as he strode across the room where she was sitting, he felt four pairs of eyes on him. Only then did he notice the other women, all in various stages of pregnancy, watching him. He leaned over, kissed Lily lightly, then took the empty seat beside her.

"I told you you didn't have to come. I know how busy you are at work."

"I wanted to come, and you're more important to me than work. Besides I'm the boss. If I want to play hooky for a few hours, I can."

Her lips twitched. Then she looked over at the two bags he'd set down beside them. Her eyes narrowed suspiciously. "What's that?"

Before he could answer, the door opened. "Mrs. Cartwright," the nurse called.

Lily rose. So did he. "Is it okay if my husband comes in with me?"

"Of course," the blond nurse with the name tag that read Sissy said with a smile. She led them down the hall and opened the door to one of the patient rooms. "You can go ahead and get undressed. Dr. Robinson will be with you in a few minutes."

Once Lily was in the hospital gown and seated on the examining-room table with a sheet draped over her, she said, "You never did answer my question. What's in the bags? And you'd better not tell me it's another gift for me."

"Okay, I won't tell you it's a gift for you," he told her. He'd given her a scarf for their one-week anniversary. Granted it had been a designer scarf with a respectable price tag on it because of the logo, but he had bought it because it reminded him of her. Judging from her flustered reaction, gifts weren't something Lily was used to receiving. He intended to change that. He handed her the smaller of the two bags.

"Jack, you don't have to buy me things," she told him as she took the bag.

"I like buying you things. Besides it's just a little something. I was passing the store window, saw it and thought you might like it."

She removed the jeweler's box from the bed of tissues in the bag and opened it. "Oh, Jack, it's beautiful," she said as she stared at the platinum pin. It was shaped like a lily with a diamond for the bloom's center, and Jack had taken one look at it and known it was meant for Lily. When she looked up at him again, tears swam in her eyes. "Thank you."

"You're welcome," he said and kissed her gently before handing her the other bag. "This one is for the baby."

She'd managed to blink back the threatening tears as she took the bag bearing the toy store's logo from him. "I suppose you just happened to be walking by this window, too?"

"I'll take the fifth on that one. Go ahead and open it."

She dug through the mounds of tissue and pulled out the

tiny football. "You do realize the baby might be a girl, don't you?" she asked, amusement in her voice.

"Who says our daughter can't play football?" he teased. "Besides, I've got that covered. There's another gift in the bag."

Lily pulled out the tiny pink ballet slippers and she laughed. "I can see it now, our daughter running down the football field in ballet slippers to catch a pass."

He laughed. And dear God, he thought, how he loved to see Lily laugh. Unable to resist, he kissed her. And as always, he felt that fullness in his chest and the sense that this was right. They were right together. He'd never considered himself a romantic person who believed in things like fate. He'd always believed he was responsible for his own fate. But he couldn't help thinking that somehow he and Lily were meant to be together.

At the sound of a throat clearing, they broke apart. "Good morning," Dr. Robinson said as she closed the door behind her. After introductions were made and Lily had been examined, the doctor put down her stethoscope. "Everything looks fine, Lily. I'm going to go ahead and do an ultrasound to see how your little one's doing."

Jack watched in fascination as the doctor moved the wand over Lily's belly and pointed out the baby on the screen. "Is that a leg?" he asked.

Dr. Robinson laughed. "Yes. And those are the arms," she pointed out. "Do you want to know the baby's sex?"

"Yes. No. I don't know," Lily said and looked over at him.

"It's up to you," he told her. "If you'd rather wait, it's all right with me."

"I think I want to wait."

"Then we'll wait," Jack said.

The doctor smiled. "I'll print you a copy of this," she told them. "It'll be your first picture of the baby."

An hour later, seated across a restaurant table from Lily, Jack was marveling at the baby's first picture and mulling over whether he should have it framed. "What do you think? Am I crazy?"

"No. And I think it's so sweet of you."

He winced. "There's that word *sweet* again. You keep calling me that and you're going to ruin my reputation as a tough lawyer."

"All right, Mr. Tough-Guy Lawyer, I think having it framed is very macho."

Jack laughed. "Tell you what. I know you need to get back to your office and I have to be in court this afternoon. So what do you say to having lunch with me again tomorrow and we'll go by Color and see about getting it framed?" he asked, referring to the chic gallery run by Emma Dearborn.

"Oh, Jack, I would love to. But you remember Felicity Farnsworth, the wedding planner, who helped plan our wedding?" When he nodded, she continued, "Well, she asked me to have lunch with her and a few of her friends at the country club tomorrow and I already agreed to go."

"No problem. We'll do it another time," he told her and motioned to the waiter to bring a check. "You enjoy yourself with the Debs Club."

"The Debs Club?"

He grinned. "Well, that's what everyone in Eastwick calls them. I'm not sure who came up with the name. But I think it started years ago when they were presented as debutantes at the Eastwick Cotillion. There's five of them and, with the exception of Vanessa Thorpe, they all went to school and were introduced to society together. You never saw one of them without the other, so people starting calling them the Debs Club. They meet at the club on a regular basis for lunch, always at the same table and always in the Emerald Room."

"Who else is in this club besides Felicity?" she asked. "And why would they want me to have lunch with them?"

"In answer to your first question, there's Abby Talbot, Bunny Baldwin's daughter whom you know already. Then there's Emma Dearborn who owns Color and is engaged to Reed Kelly. Mary Duvall who's a local artist and Vanessa Thorpe, Stuart Thorpe's widow," he told her. "As to your second question, I imagine they want you to join them for lunch because Felicity told them what a remarkable woman you are."

"I think you might be a little biased."

"Not at all. Just stating the facts," he told her. "You should enjoy yourself and the food at the club is excellent."

"I know. I met Bunny there once for lunch when she couldn't come by the Eastwick Cares offices." She paused, furrowed her brow. "I didn't ask, but I'm assuming Felicity will leave my name at the gate so the guard will let me through. Last time, Bunny forgot and I was late meeting her because I wasn't on the list."

"Lily, you don't need anyone to put your name on a guest list. You're my wife. That means you're a member of the East-wick Country Club now. The club membership, the boat, our house, it's all yours, too."

"You're very generous."

"We're married. Married people share." He paused, decided to broach the issue of her apartment again. "Speaking of sharing, I thought maybe we could go by your apartment this weekend and see about moving the rest of your things."

"I told you, I doubt my stuff will fit in with your things. Besides there's no hurry. My lease runs for another six months. Let's just see how things go." She glanced at her watch. "Look at the time! I'd better get back to the office. I have an appointment and you need to get to court."

Disappointed, he tossed some bills on the table and walked

with Lily to her car. He wished he knew how to convince her that their marriage wasn't temporary, that *he* wasn't temporary. Because he knew in his gut that's why she was holding back. It was the reason she insisted on keeping the apartment. She didn't trust him.

"Thanks again for coming to the doctor's office and for the beautiful pin. I'll see you tonight.

"Lily, you forgot something," he told her when she started to get in the car.

"What?"

"This." He hauled her into his arms and kissed her right then and there. Ignoring the whoops from the construction crew on the corner, he gave her a real kiss—one that involved mouths and teeth and tongues. When he lifted his head, she had a dazed expression in her eyes. Good, he thought and turned around and walked away.

Nine

"Thank you," Lily told the waiter as he refilled her iced tea. She looked around the Emerald Room of the Eastwick Country Club. She could see where it got its name, she decided, noting the Irish green color of the decor and the malachite bar. Looking past the open French doors, she gazed out at the pool area. Everything was green and bright and springlike. The pink-and-white blossoms of the mountain laurel were a shock of color against the lawn and trees. And even from her seat inside the club, she could smell the sweet fragrance from the colorful shrubs. She noted the tiny white lights strung through the tree branches and imagined it must be beautiful out on the patio area in the moonlight. For a moment, she could almost see herself and Jack out there, dancing under the starlight.

"You decided on a dessert yet, Lily?" Felicity asked.

At the sound of her name, Lily yanked her attention back

to the lunch table and picked the first thing on the menu. "The cheesecake with strawberries, please."

While the waiter continued to take their orders, she glanced around at her lunch companions. They were all so different, she thought. And every one of them was beautiful. Tall, slender with sleek black hair and violet eyes, Emma Dearborn was stunning. She was also a sharp contrast to the delicate beauty of Vanessa Thorpe whose petite frame and pale blond hair gave her an air of innocence. Lily knew from Jack that Vanessa was already a widow. Mary Duvall had a quieter beauty with her brown bob and soft brown eyes. Yet there was a mysterious air about her that Lily suspected came from being an artist and from living in Europe. Felicity was her bubbly self and she had turned more than one head when she'd walked into the club. Lily wasn't sure if it was the other woman's voluptuous figure and spiky blond hair or her fearless attitude. With lovely blue eyes and long blond hair, Abby was the classic beauty. Although Lily guessed Abby to be slightly shorter than her own five-foot-six-inch frame, the other woman was petite and carried herself with a grace that a person was born with and could never be learned. There was a sadness about Abby that called out to her, Lily thought, and she surmised the other woman was still grieving for her mother.

Once the waiter was gone, Emma leaned closer and said, "Okay, Lily, as you can see we desperately need you on the country club's fund-raising committee. From everything that Felicity told me about you and after talking to Mrs. Cartwright about your work with Eastwick Cares, we all think you'd be great on the committee."

"She's right, Lily," Abby added. "My mother always spoke so highly of you. She said that it wasn't until you came to work at Eastwick Cares that the agency really saw any significant success with their fund-raisers."

"That was very kind of her," Lily said. "And it was kind of all of you to ask me. I'm not sure how much help I'll be, but the answer's yes. I'd love to be on the committee."

"One more thing," Emma said. "You've probably heard that the five of us are called the Debs Club."

"As a matter of fact, I did," Lily told her.

"It's okay," Emma laughed. "We don't mind. In fact, we refer to ourselves by that name now. The truth is we're just five women with very busy lives who are friends. We try to get together about once a month for a girls-only lunch where we can celebrate, complain or just hang out with each other."

"It sounds nice."

"We were hoping you'd say that, weren't we ladies?" They all nodded. "We want you to join our little club, Lily," Emma told her.

Surprised, Lily responded, "I don't know what to say."

"Say yes," Abby told her.

"Yes," she repeated and they all laughed.

"Okay, ladies. I think this deserves a toast," Felicity said and raised her glass. "To Lily Cartwright, the newest member of the Eastwick Country Club's Fund-raising Committee and the newest addition to the Debs Club."

Glasses clinked all around. As they chatted and sampled each other's desserts, Lily found herself enjoying her new friends. She almost felt as though she really did belong. It made her begin to believe that miracles were possible. Maybe someday Jack would love her the way she loved him.

A voluptuous blonde with a rock the size of Texas on her finger stopped in front of their table. "Hello, ladies. It looks like you girls are having a celebration."

"Hello, Delia. And yes, we are having a celebration," Emma said cooly. "Lily just became a member of the Debs Club."

"Congratulations," Delia said and the woman's smile was as phony as her dye job. "I'm Delia Forrester, by the way."

"How do you do?" Lily responded politely and shook the other woman's hand. "I'm Lily Miller…um, Cartwright."

Delia looked at Lily's belly. "Then you must be Jack Cartwright's new bride."

"Yes, I am."

"What a lucky girl you are. Jack is such a *wonderful* man," she said in a way that made Lily wonder just how well Delia Forrester knew him. "Do give him my best."

"Of course," Lily said and resumed her seat. But she couldn't shake the image of Delia with Jack out of her head. "Who is she?"

"Frank Forrester's trophy wife," Felicity told her and it was clear from her tone that she didn't care for Delia. Lily couldn't say that she cared much for her either.

"Okay, now where were we?" Felicity asked.

"We were toasting our newest Deb," Abby told her.

"Maybe we should take out a notice in the newspapers, announcing that Lily is now officially a member of the Debs Club," Felicity joked.

"Wouldn't that set tongues to wagging," Vanessa said with a smile.

"If only your mom were still alive, Abby," Emma began. "Bunny was the one who knew everything about everyone. So if you wanted to know what was happening in Eastwick, like Lily becoming a member of the Debs Club, all you had to do was pick up her *Social Diary.*"

Abby smiled, but there was a sadness behind it. There was also something else in her eyes. But before Lily could decipher it, Abby said, "Mother always used to say that if she had been around in Hedda Hopper's and Louella Parsons' heyday, she'd have given them a run for their money."

"And she was right," Felicity added.

"I know you said you were too upset when Bunny first died even to think about starting up the *Diary* again," Emma remarked. "Have you given it any more thought?"

"Actually, it's one of the reasons I was glad we were meeting today. You remember how my mother was so mysterious about her sources and kept a journal with her notes about her scoops for the *Social Diary* in her safe?"

"Sure," Emma said. And they all nodded in agreement.

"Well, last week I finally started going through Mother's things," Abby continued. "Only, when I opened the safe where she kept her journals, it was empty. Someone has stolen her journals."

"Are you serious?" Felicity asked.

Abby nodded.

"But who? Why?" Lily asked.

"I don't know. But I've asked the police to open a new inquest into Mother's death. I don't think she died of a heart attack. I think she was murdered," Abby declared.

"Murdered?" Mary repeated and brought her hand to her throat.

"Yes. I think something in her journals may have gotten Mother killed."

Lily shivered at the idea. "I'm sorry, Abby. I can't imagine how hard this must be for you."

"Thanks," she replied. "I just wanted all of you to know because the police are probably going to be questioning people and they might question you."

Mary tipped over her glass and it spilled, catching the skirt of Lily's dress. "I'm so sorry," Mary began and started blotting at the dress with a napkin. "I can't believe what a klutz I am."

"It's okay," Lily told her. "Really, it's fine."

"Oh, gosh, look at the time," Emma declared. "I need to

run. I'm supposed to be meeting a client at the gallery in ten minutes."

"Emma, did you forget you're supposed to meet with me after lunch so you can select a wedding cake today? Not to mention you're supposed to choose the napkins and pick out the music," Felicity protested.

"I'm sorry," Emma said and grabbed her purse. "Why don't you just meet with Reed and you and he decide."

"But, Emma, this is *your* wedding, not mine. You should be the one making these decisions with Reed, not me."

"I know. But the truth is I don't have time and Reed thinks you're terrific. He's always raving about what a good job you're doing. So the two of you work it out. Now I've got to run," Emma said. "Lily, I'm thrilled to have you as a Deb and I'll be in touch about the fund-raising." And before anyone could respond, Emma disappeared, practically running on her stiletto heels.

"Did it come out?" Mary asked her, referring to the tea stain on her dress.

"Not yet. I'll just go to the ladies' room and use a little soap on it. Don't worry. I've survived hundreds of spills. This one isn't bad at all."

The spill really hadn't been that bad, Lily thought as she surveyed her cleaning job in the mirror of the ladies' room. Deciding she'd better use the facilities now instead of making another trip in thirty minutes, Lily disappeared into one of the stalls.

The swish of the door to the powder room opening was followed by the clicking of women's heels on the marble floor. "I just need to freshen my lipstick," a woman said and Lily immediately recognized the voice of Delia Forrester.

"Well, I need to potty. I knew I shouldn't have had that second Bloody Mary," another woman complained and Lily heard the door to one of the other bathroom stalls open and close.

"Patty, did you happen to get a look at the new addition at the Debs Club's table?"

"You mean the pregnant little redhead?"

"Yes," Delia said. "She's Jack Cartwright's new wife. And now we all know why the rush-rush wedding, don't we?"

"You're kidding! A shotgun wedding?" the woman named Patty remarked. A toilet flushed and the other woman exited the stall.

"I hear she's a little nobody. You'd think a man in Jack's position would be a little more selective about who he sleeps with," Delia said. "What is it they say, if you sleep with dogs, you're bound to get fleas? Well, I guess it's true. No wonder he decided not to run for the senate. With that wife of his as baggage, he probably wouldn't get elected dogcatcher."

Having heard enough, Lily exited her stall and walked over to the sinks where the other two women were laughing. She took the spot between them and proceeded to wash her hands. The woman named Patty immediately sobered. Delia had a smug smile on her lips. And when Lily met the other woman's eyes in the mirror, she realized that Delia had known she was there all along. Reaching for one of the cloth towels, Lily dried her hands and disposed of the towel in the used laundry receptacle.

She started toward the door, stopped, turned. "Oh, by the way. You ladies really shouldn't worry about whether or not my husband could get elected as dogcatcher. He doesn't need the job. In case you haven't heard, he's filthy rich."

And without waiting for them to respond, Lily left the bathroom. But despite her bravado, she could feel her stomach pitching. Once she was out of sight, she leaned against the wall and squeezed her eyes shut a moment. She loved Jack and the last thing she ever wanted to do was to bring him down.

"Lily? Are you all right?"

Lily opened her eyes at the sound of Abby's voice. "Yes, I'm fine."

"The rest of the girls had to leave and said to tell you good-bye."

"You didn't have to wait for me," Lily told her.

"I wanted to. Besides I thought I saw Delia go into the bath-room behind you," Abby explained and glanced in the direction of the ladies' room. "I was worried she might have cornered you and tried to wheedle an invitation or something out of you."

"No. No, she didn't," Lily told her. "But thanks for check-ing on me."

"It wasn't a big deal," Abby told her as they walked down the corridor. When they reached the Emerald Room, Abby said, "There's another exit through here."

The moment they stepped outdoors into the patio area near the pool the sweet scent of the mountain laurel sur-rounded them.

"My mother liked you a lot," Abby told her. "She spoke very highly of you."

Once again, Lily was struck with empathy for Abby and it helped her push aside her own concerns. "I thought the world of her, too. In fact, it's because of her that I met Jack." Lily told her about Bunny insisting she come to the ball, about lending her the dress, about meeting Jack at the ball.

"My mother loved happy endings. I think she would be pleased to know that she's responsible for you two finding yours," Abby told her.

"Abby, you don't have to pretend. I'm sure everyone knows that the only reason Jack married me was because of the baby."

"And you married him because you love him."

Lily sighed. "Is it that obvious?"

"Only to someone who suffers from the same disease."

"It's different for you, though. You and your husband married because you love one another," Lily told her.

"I thought we did. At least it's the reason I married Luke," Abby told her. "I'm not sure anymore why Luke married me."

"I'm sure he loves you," Lily offered, wanting to comfort her new friend.

"Maybe. But loving someone is a lot more than just saying the words. From what I've heard, Jack sure acts like a man who's in love."

Maybe Abby was right, Lily told herself. At least she hoped she was.

Jack strode into the bar of the Eastwick Country Club and scanned the room for Tom Carlton.

"Jack, over here."

Jack headed over to the bar where Tom sat on a stool, sipping a glass of bourbon. At sixty-five, Tom was short and stocky with a receding hairline and a firm handshake. His mild appearance belied the fact that he was a shark and one of the biggest political power brokers in the state. Jack offered his hand. "Good to see you, Tom."

"You, too," Tom said with a slap on Jack's back. "What's your poison?"

"I'll just have a ginger ale, Harry," Jack advised the bartender who had been a fixture at the club since Jack had been a boy. Somewhere between sixty and seventy, Harry was tall, bald and silent. While people always said, "If these walls could talk," he imagined Harry could tell the walls a thing or two.

"Ginger ale?" Carlton repeated. "I thought you were a scotch man."

"Right now I'm a married man whose wife is expecting a baby. Thanks, Harry," he said when the glass was placed in front of him. "Lily's drink of choice is milk and occasionally juice these days. I've changed my drinking habits so that they're more in line with hers."

Carlton shook his head. "I guess that's just one more of the changes in today's society. During my generation, a man wasn't expected to change his eating and drinking habits because his wife was pregnant."

"It's a personal decision. But I'm sure you didn't ask me to meet you to discuss my eating and drinking habits. What's on your mind, Tom?"

"That's what I like about you, Cartwright. You're direct."

"I find it saves time. And time isn't something I have a lot to spare these days," he informed him. It was true. Between work and his commitments to his family and the community, his time had always been in short supply. Now that he was married to Lily he'd discovered he wanted more time with her and he suspected he would want even more once the baby arrived.

"Why don't we go have a seat over there, where we can have a little more privacy," Tom suggested, indicating a table in the far corner of the bar. Once they were both seated, Carlton said, "You wanted me to be direct. So I'll get straight to the point. I want you to reconsider running for Peterson's senate seat."

"Tom—"

He held up his hand. "Let me finish. The preliminary test polls I had my people run show the seat is yours for the taking." He leaned forward, "Jack, you could be the next senator of Connecticut. Think of all the good you could do, the legislation you could introduce. You would make a difference in a lot of people's lives. And you'd certainly be doing the city of Eastwick proud. All you've got to do is give me the word and we kick off your campaign tomorrow."

"I appreciate the offer. Honestly I do. And while I do have

a lot of ideas about how to make this country run better, now is not the right time for me to try to do it. Maybe at some time in the future, but not now."

"Listen, Jack. I understand your reservations. And when I found out the real reason you pulled out, I agreed with your decision."

"The real reason I pulled out?" Jack repeated because he'd thought he'd made it clear that the reason he decided not to run was because he didn't want to subject himself or Lily to the time and commitment running a political race would demand.

"Your quickie marriage to this Miller girl because you got her pregnant," Tom answered matter-of-factly. "Politically, I figured it would be a nail in your coffin the same as you did. I mean the people of Connecticut place a lot of stock in family values. They expect a man and woman to get married first and then make babies. But I was wrong," Carlton told him proudly. "You doing the honorable thing and marrying the girl, well, that made you a stand-up guy in the voters' eyes."

"Did it now?" Jack asked softly while he tried to keep his anger in check.

"It sure did. And if you're worried that your wife's background will be a problem, it won't. The PR team thinks her growing up in an orphanage and foster homes, having to work to make something of herself will work in your favor. The voters will see you as a senator for the common man as well as the rich." Beaming, Carlton asked, "So what do you say? Do we start printing the Cartwright for Senate bumper stickers?"

"No," Jack said between gritted teeth.

"No? Did you just hear what I said? You're a shoo-in to be the next senator of Connecticut."

"I heard you. And I'm not interested." Jack stood.

"Why the hell not?"

"First off, because I don't have any use for narrow-minded bigots and I certainly wouldn't want one running my campaign—if I had a campaign to run. Secondly, because I don't want to take time I could be spending with my wife and baby to jump on the political merry-go-round." Jack shoved his chair back and ignoring the stir of voices behind him, he continued. "And just to set the record straight, Carlton, if I ever do decide to run for political office, I'll want Lily standing by my side all right. But it won't be because she makes for good copy. It'll be because I'm proud of who she is, of what she's done, and I'm feel damn lucky to have her as my wife. Now if you'll excuse me, I don't much care for the stench in here." And before he gave in to the urge to plant his fist in Carlton's face, Jack left the bar.

So intent was he on leaving the country club that he nearly barreled into Abby Talbot who was on her way down the corridor. "Sorry, Abby. I didn't see you."

"That much was obvious. So where's the fire?" she asked and smiled.

"No fire. I'm just on my way home."

She looked behind him. "Is Lily not with you?"

"No," Jack told her, his mood softening at the mention of Lily's name. "She's at home. That's why I was in a hurry."

"I understand," Abby told him. "She's lovely, Jack."

"I think so, too. And I wanted to thank you for asking her to join the Debs Club. It meant a lot to her. I'm afraid marrying into the Cartwright family hasn't been all that easy for her. Suddenly she's under a microscope, being judged, trying to live up to what she thinks is expected of her. You asking her to be on the fund-raising committee and to join your club, I think it made her feel like…like less of an outsider."

"I know," Abby told him. "For what it's worth, I think she's pretty special and you're darned lucky she married you."

"I think so, too." When he noted Abby looking in the direction of the entrance, Jack glanced behind him, then asked, "Are you looking for someone?"

She flushed. "I'm waiting for Luke. He's been in New York on business since last week and wasn't due back until tomorrow, but he was able to wrap things up early. He's driving straight here from the airport so we can have dinner and then take in a movie together," she explained.

"Sounds like a fun evening." And it also explained why Abby was wearing the sexy black dress and smiling for the first time in weeks.

"It should be. Luke and I haven't been out to dinner or a movie together since…well, since longer than I can remember." Her cell phone rang.

"I'll let you get that."

"No, just a sec," she said, and opening her evening bag, she pulled out the cell phone and frowned. Turning her body to the side, she answered, "Hello." Her expression changed from one of joy to one of total despair as she listened. "I see. I'm sure you are. No, don't bother," she said and ended the call.

"Everything all right?" he asked even though it was obvious it wasn't.

"I guess that depends on who you ask," she said, a note of bitterness in her voice. "I'm sorry, Jack. I didn't mean to snap at you. That was Luke canceling our date. He couldn't get away after all."

"I'm sorry, Abby."

"So am I," she said. "A word of advice from a married woman, Jack. Whatever you do, you make time for Lily, and make sure that a day doesn't go by that she doesn't know that you love her."

Lily checked her appearance in the mirror one last time. The saleswoman at the dress shop had called it the Audrey

Hepburn little black dress for pregnant women. Lily turned, looked over her shoulder at her image. From the back, the dress did look perfect, she admitted. It showed a nice amount of leg, made her hips look slim and you couldn't even tell she was pregnant—until she turned around. She sighed. Still, the neckline was a bit daring and her baby bump…well, it couldn't be helped. She was nearly six months pregnant and there was simply no hiding her little soccer ball.

When Jack had suggested they have dinner to celebrate their three-week anniversary, she had been excited. There had been a change in him this past week. While he was always thoughtful and generous and left her with no doubt about his desire for her, there had been an urgency, an intensity in his lovemaking that she was sure would not be possible if he didn't love her. Following her encounter with Delia Forrester she had questioned him about why he had withdrawn his name for consideration in the senate race, and he had made it clear that his decision was a selfish one—he wanted the time with her and their baby.

Today when he'd left, he'd been so mysterious about tonight. She'd learned enough about Jack in the few weeks since they had been married to realize that the man loved surprising her with little gifts. She'd lost count of them there had been so many— some silly, some horribly expensive. Whatever his surprise was tonight, it was one he was excited about. So she was excited, too.

Lily checked the seams of her stocking and told herself that the three-inch heels were worth it. They made her legs look a mile long. Walking over to the vanity, she picked up her locket and put it on. After fastening the clasp, she smoothed the ends of the up-do again. She picked up the scarlet lipstick, slicked it on her lips, pressed them together.

Enough, Lily. You're acting like a schoolgirl going to the prom.

She laughed at herself. In a lot of ways, she felt like a schoolgirl. And it was Jack's fault. The man made her feel like a princess and she had never been so happy in her life. Suddenly the panic she'd always felt when she thought things were too good to be true sneaked its way into her thoughts.

Don't get too comfortable. If you do, when it all crashes down around you, there'll be no one to help put you back together.

No, Lily told herself. She wasn't going to do this to herself. She was happy. Jack was happy. They loved one another. All right, so he hadn't said the words. But Abby was right, he showed he loved her by his actions. She didn't need the words.

Grabbing her evening bag, she headed downstairs to wait for Jack. But when twenty minutes passed, she checked her watch. He'd said the dinner reservations were for eight o'clock. It was already seven-twenty. Five more minutes. If he wasn't home, she'd call him.

But she'd no sooner made the decision when the phone rang. Lily snatched it up. "Jack, where are you?"

"I'm sorry, sweetheart. I got tied up at the office. The guy I'm meeting with is running late. I'd cancel, but he's come from out of town just to meet with me."

"I understand," she said and tried to keep the disappointment out of her voice. "I'll just call and cancel the reservation."

"No. That's not what I want—"

"But you're tied up. We'll just go another time."

"Tonight's our anniversary. I want to have dinner and go dancing with my wife tonight," he told her and the tone of his voice sent longing through her.

"I'd like that, too. But you said this poor man has traveled from out of town just to meet with you. You can hardly cancel on him."

"I don't intend to. He should be here at any time now. If

you wouldn't mind driving yourself to the restaurant, I'll meet you there. What do you say?"

"I say it sounds like a plan."

"Great. I'll see you there. Order us some mozzarella cheese sticks," he said.

"All right. And, Jack?"

"Yes?"

"I love you."

"You'd better. You're married to me, lady," he joked. "See you in a bit."

"Bye," Lily said and hung up the phone. For a moment, she found herself disappointed. She'd deliberately told him she loved him when they weren't in bed, hoping that with passion out of the mix, he might tell her. He hadn't. Suddenly, she could feel the old doubt surfacing again.

Stop it, Lily told herself, and snatching her car keys from the table in the foyer, she pulled open the front door.

Thunder rumbled in the distance. A light rain had already begun to fall. Going back inside, she pulled open the coat closet to get her raincoat—then realized it was still at her apartment. Lily looked down at her beautiful, price-of-a-week's-salary dress, and had visions of arriving at the restaurant looking like a drowned rat.

Then she spied Jack's raincoat. Removing it from the hanger, she slipped it on and grinned. It worked much better than her raincoat, she thought. It covered all of her. After belting it, she slid her hands into the pocket.

Her fingers brushed a wad of paper. Pulling it out, she walked over to the table. She smoothed it out and her stomach dropped as she read:

WHAT WOULD THE GOOD CITIZENS OF EAST-WICK THINK IF THEY FOUND OUT THAT THEIR

CANDIDATE FOR THE SENATE WAS ABOUT TO
BECOME AN UNWED FATHER?

UNLESS YOU WANT EVERYONE TO KNOW
YOUR DIRTY LITTLE SECRET, YOU'LL PLACE
$50,000 IN SMALL BILLS IN A SHOPPING BAG
AND LEAVE IT IN EASTWICK PARK UNDER THE
BENCH ACROSS FROM THE FOUNTAIN BY
NOON TOMORROW. IF YOU FAIL TO DELIVER
THE MONEY OR NOTIFY THE AUTHORITIES,
YOU CAN FORGET THE SENATE NOMINATION.

Lily dropped the note to the floor. Suddenly everything
came rushing back. Delia's comments at the club, Jack telling
her he had opted out of the senate race to be with her. Jack
never saying he loved her.

Oh, God, she thought. Oh, God, she was going to be sick.
She raced to the bathroom, threw up. When it was finally
over, she took a wet towel, wiped her face. And when she
looked at the face of the woman in the mirror, she recognized
her, saw through all the pretenses, all the lies she'd told herself. She was still the same person she'd always been—Lily
Miller. The baby her own mother hadn't wanted, the girl no
family ever wanted to adopt. The woman Jack Cartwright
would never love.

Crying, she raced up the stairs, fell, picked herself up and
continued to the top. She went into the bedroom, threw some
of her clothes in a suitcase, grabbed Bentley, and then she
raced downstairs. Taking off Jack's raincoat, she threw it to
the floor and went out into the rain. She had to get away, go
far away where she would never have to face Jack again.

By the time she got into the car and onto the main road,
the rain was coming down like a flood. So were her tears. She
continued to speed down the road, not even bothering to slow

down in the turn. All she could see was that note, Jack's face, realize how wrong she had been.

Between the driving rain and her non-stop tears, she could barely see through the windshield, Lily realized. Reaching over, she dug through her bag for a tissue to wipe the fog on the windshield inside the car.

And when she looked up again, she saw the lights coming at her, heard the screech of tires, the sound of glass breaking, the crunch of metal. Lily grabbed her stomach. "My baby," she cried out. Then everything went black.

Ten

Jack stood at the reception desk of Vincent's, the Italian restaurant where Lily was supposed to meet him, and waited to be shown to his table. He was nearly half an hour late, but he hoped Lily would think the wait was worth it. He patted the pocket where he had a slip of paper with the name of a woman who claimed to have known Lily's mother. It had taken weeks, but after providing a picture of Lily's locket and what little information he had about Lily's abandonment at the church, the detective he'd hired had finally been able to get a solid lead. Jack had wanted to do this for her because he hoped that if she had those answers to her past she might be able to let it go.

It might be selfish of him, but he wanted all of Lily. She'd told him she loved him and he didn't doubt she did. But there was that piece of her heart that she held back, held back, he was sure, because she was afraid to trust him. He understood it, didn't blame her. She'd been let down too many times in the past.

He didn't intend to let her down. But he needed her to believe in him, to believe in them. And to do that, she would have to find those answers to her past that had plagued her all of her life.

"Mr. Cartwright, it is good to see you again," Antonio, the maître d' told him. "We have your table ready for you. Would you like to be seated now or do you want to wait for Mrs. Cartwright?"

Jack frowned. "Isn't my wife here?"

Antonio looked at the hostess. "Has Mrs. Cartwright arrived?"

"No, sir."

"I am sorry, she is not here yet," Antonio said. "Perhaps she got caught in traffic. You know how the rain slows things down."

"Could you check to see if she called and left a message? She was supposed to meet me here at eight," Jack explained.

"Of course, I'll see if anyone took a call from her. One moment."

While Antonio went to check to see if Lily had called, Jack pulled out his cell phone. He hit number one, where he had programmed in Lily's cell number. On the fourth ring, she answered, "Hello. This is Lily—"

"Lily," Jack began only to realize he'd reached her voice mail. "Lily, I'm at Vincent's. Where are you? Call me." After ending the call, he tried the house, telling himself that maybe she'd got tied up at home. But once again, he got the answering machine.

"I'm sorry, Mr. Cartwright. But none of the staff have heard from Mrs. Cartwright. Would you like to have a drink in the bar while you wait for her?"

"Thanks, Antonio. But I'll just wait here. I'm sure she'll be along any minute now."

But twenty minutes and a string of phone messages later,

Lily still hadn't arrived. And Jack began to worry. It wasn't like Lily to be late and it certainly wasn't like her not to respond to phone calls. Because of her pregnancy, she was especially diligent about never being incommunicado. Something was wrong.

After tipping Antonio and apologizing for canceling the dinner reservation, Jack left the restaurant and started for home. During the drive, he continued to try Lily's cell number and even tried her office. Growing more worried by the mile, he tried Abby Talbot. He knew that Lily had become close to the other woman.

"Hello," she answered on the second ring.

"Abby, it's Jack Cartwright."

"Jack," she said and judging by the disappointment in her voice, she had been expecting someone else's call. "What can I do for you?"

"I'm sorry to bother you this late. But I was wondering if Lily was with you."

"Lily?" she repeated. "No. I haven't seen her since earlier today. I went shopping with her. She said you and she had a special evening planned and she wanted a new dress for the occasion. I thought she was with you."

"No, she isn't," he said and turned onto the interstate and headed toward home. "I was running late and she was supposed to meet me at the restaurant. But she never showed."

"I guess you tried her cell."

"Yes. I keep getting her voice mail. And she's not answering at home or her office."

"You know how pregnant women are, they fall asleep at the drop of a hat. She might just be taking a nap and turned off the phone," Abby offered.

Which they both knew wasn't the case, Jack thought, but appreciated that the other woman was trying to reassure him.

"I'm on my way home now. Would you mind calling the rest of the Debs Club and see if any of them have heard from her?"

"Sure. I'll do it right away."

"Thanks."

"No problem. And, Jack, try not to worry. Lily's one of the strongest and bravest women I know. I'm sure wherever she is, she's fine. Nothing short of wild horses would have kept her away from meeting you for that dinner tonight."

"I'm sure you're right," Jack said. But as he hung up the phone he was worried that something a lot more serious than wild horses had stopped her from meeting him.

A call to his parents and both his sisters rendered the same results. No one had seen or heard from Lily. And by the time he exited the interstate, he had a sick feeling in his gut. All sorts of images were racing through his head. What if Lily had fallen? What if she had slipped in the bathtub? Suppose she had gone into labor early? He'd read about it, knew that it was more common than people realized. She was nearly six months pregnant. He never should have left her alone.

Realizing he was sending himself into a panic, Jack forced himself to calm down. He tried to recall their last conversation and whether there had been anything out of the ordinary. He hadn't detected anything wrong. On the contrary, she had sounded happy. And she had told him that she loved him. Hardly the actions of a woman who was upset with him. So where was she?

Jack steered his Mercedes into the sharp turn, then hit the gas for the long stretch of road that led to his home. When he pulled up to the house, the first thing he noticed was that her car was gone. Which meant Lily wasn't there. Maybe she'd left him a note, Jack thought, even though he knew the probabilities were slim. Why would she leave him a note instead of calling?

Still when he opened the door and entered the foyer, he was

struck by the silence. "Lily?" he called out. But there was no answer. Tossing his keys on the table near the door, he headed into the house. He turned the corner into the living room and saw his raincoat lying on the floor. Walking over, he picked up the coat and as he did so, he saw the slip of paper on the ground.

Jack froze. Reaching down, he picked up the buff-colored note—the blackmail note that he had shoved into his coat pocket and forgotten about because he had dismissed it. He read the ugly words again and tried to imagine what Lily had thought when she'd read them.

She would have thought that he had lied to her, that he had opted out of the senate race because he was ashamed of her.

"Son of a—" Jack crushed the note in his fist. He had to find Lily. He had to explain. He was racing toward the door when his cell phone rang. He didn't even bother to look at the caller ID. He simply said, "Lily?"

"No, Jack. It's Scott."

"Listen, Scott. I don't have time right now. Lily's missing and I'm on my way to look for her," he explained and jumped behind the wheel of the car.

"Jack, it's Lily I'm calling about."

Something in his old friend's voice made Jack's heart stop. Panic ripped through his blood. "What the hell is it, Scott? Where's my wife?"

"She's at Eastwick Memorial Hospital. There was an accident."

"Oh, God." Jack could feel a thundering in his head. Or was it his soul? He wasn't sure. All he knew was that he couldn't imagine a life without Lily. "How bad is she?"

"She's in a coma. You need to get here as soon as you can."

Jack wasn't sure how many speeding violations or driving infractions he committed. All he knew was that he made it to the hospital in record time and ignored the security guard telling him he couldn't leave his car parked at the entrance as he raced to the front desk. "Lily Cartwright? Which room is she in?"

"She's in room 302. But I'm afraid visiting hours are over, sir—"

Jack ran to the elevator bank, punched the button. Then went to the stairwell. He raced up the three flights and when he barreled through the stairwell exit door, he nearly mowed down a nurse's aide. "Sorry," he said as he continued running to the nurses' station. "Room 302. Lily Cartwright? Which way is it?"

"It's down the end of that hall and to the right," the uniformed nurse told him. "But you'll need—"

Jack didn't hear the rest. He zipped down the hall, hung a right and started toward the room at the far end.

"Jack! Jack," Scott called after him as he sped past the family waiting room.

Jack stopped long enough to say, "I've got to see her, Scott. I've got to explain."

"Hang on, buddy. You'll have plenty of time to explain when she wakes up."

"I need to see her."

"Come on, I'll go with you," Scott said and walked with him to Lily's room.

When he opened the door and saw Lily, Jack could feel tears stinging his eyes. He walked over to the bed, held her hand. It was cold. She was deathly pale. There was a bruise on her forehead, scratches on her face and arms, a bandage above her left eyebrow. There were monitors attached to her and an IV in her arm. In that moment, Jack would have given everything he owned, his very life, just to see her open those ghost-blue eyes and look at him.

Scott clamped a hand on his shoulder. "You all right?"

Jack nodded. "What happened?"

"I'm not sure. From what I was able to get from the driver of the truck that hit her, the rain was coming down so hard you could hardly see the hand in front of your face and she came tearing around a curve in the road, veered out of her lane and came straight at the truck."

It was his fault. It was his fault. She'd found the blackmail note and run out. "Where's the doctor? What does he say? What about the baby? Did she…is the baby okay?"

"The doctor's running some tests. He should be back in a few minutes. You need to stay calm, buddy. Lily's going to need you when she comes out of this."

Scott was right. Jack knew he was. "Why did they contact you?" he asked, only now realizing that it was Scott that was here with Lily when it should have been him.

"It was one of Falcon Trucking's semis that hit her," he explained. "When I was notified one of my drivers was hurt, I came down. That's when I found out the other victim was Lily. So I called you."

Jack nodded. "How bad was the accident?"

"Bad enough. It's a miracle Lily wasn't killed. My driver has a broken arm and a broken collarbone."

It was a miracle she wasn't dead. And if she had died, it would be because of him, Jack chided himself.

"Come on. Let's go get a cup of coffee while we wait for the doctor."

Four cups of coffee later, the doctor came into the waiting room. "Mr. Cartwright?"

Jack stood. "I'm Jack Cartwright."

"I'm Dr. Freeman." Tall, broad-shouldered with a head of salt-and-pepper hair, the doctor had a solid handshake. "Why don't we step outside so we can talk."

Jack followed the doctor and Scott came with him. When

they reached a separate waiting area, Jack asked, "Is my wife going to be okay?"

"Her vitals are good. Nothing's broken. She has a concussion and a nasty cut over her left eyebrow and some bruises and scrapes. But none of those are life-threatening. Our biggest concern is the coma. The longer she remains comatose, the more concerned we have to be."

"What about the baby?" Jack asked.

"The baby looks fine. We've hooked up a fetal monitor to watch the baby and I've called your wife's obstetrician, Dr. Robinson."

"Is there anything we can do in the meantime?" Jack asked.

"You might try talking to her. Sometimes a patient will respond to the voice of a loved one. And it never hurts to pray."

So Jack prayed. He prayed as he never had before, pleading with the Almighty to save her, to bring her back to him. And he talked to Lily. He told her how much he loved her, how much he needed her and about the wonderful life they were going to have together with their baby. He told her about all the other babies he wanted to make with her— babies with her red hair and his blue eyes, babies with her compassion and capacity for giving, babies who would be smarter than their father who should have told her about the blackmail note.

He wasn't sure how long he talked to her. He knew he talked until his voice grew hoarse. And that he chased both his parents and his sisters out when they came in fussing and panicked and insisting he rest. He knew that Scott never left. That Abby and the other Debs Club members had all come and kept vigil. Finally they had given up on trying to make him leave Lily and had left him alone.

Holding her hand, he pleaded again, "Please, Lily. Please come back to me. I love you. I need you. Come back."

* * *

Please, Lily. Please come back to me. I love you. I need you. Come back.

Lily could hear Jack's voice. It sounded as though it was coming to her through a tunnel. But it kept growing stronger and stronger.

Please come back to me. I love you.

Slowly Lily opened her eyes. She winced because just moving her eyelashes hurt. She touched her head, felt the bump and the bandage above her brow. She felt as if she'd been run over by a truck. And then she remembered. Finding the blackmail note. Driving in the rain and crying. The sound of tires squealing, glass breaking, the crash. And then darkness.

The baby.

Her heart skipped a beat. She touched her stomach and could breathe again when she felt the bump in her belly. Then she turned her head and saw Jack. He was seated at the side of her bed with his head down, his shoulders slumped. He had her hand buried somewhere beneath his and from the steady rise and fall of his shoulders, she suspected he was asleep. Gently she eased her hand from beneath his and she stroked his head.

Slowly he lifted his head. The eyes that looked at her were bloodshot and had dark circles beneath them. He looked as though he hadn't seen a razor for days and his hair—his usually neatly styled hair—looked as though it had been combed by a rake. But it was the torment in those eyes that broke her heart.

"The baby?" Even though her mother's heart told her that the baby was all right, she had to ask anyway. "Is the baby okay?"

"The baby's fine."

She breathed a sigh of relief. "Am I going to be all right?"

"Yes. The doctor says you should be fine. It was just the coma that gave us a scare. We didn't know if…when…you would come out of it."

"How long have I been here?"

"Since last night."

"And you've been here this whole time?" she asked.

"Of course. You're my wife. I love you. There's no place else I'd rather be than with you."

"I heard you talking to me, you know. I would feel myself start to sink and then I would hear your voice telling me to come back, not to leave you, that you loved me."

"And I do love you, Lily. I think I have since the first time I saw you at the ball. I was just too stupid and stubborn to realize it until I almost lost you. I'm so sorry," he told her. "It's my fault you were in that accident. I should have told you about the blackmail note."

"Yes, you should have." Realizing how close she had come to losing her life and her baby had wiped away the frantic need she'd felt to run away and escape the pain. Facing death had made her recognize how precious life was, how even more precious love was. To try to lock away a piece of her heart out of fear of being hurt was wrong. Not only was she cheating Jack, she was cheating herself. How could she ever expect for Jack or anyone to love her when she was unwilling to allow herself to love him the way she had always wanted to be loved—with her whole heart? And to love with her whole heart meant she needed to trust with her whole heart, too. "Why didn't you tell me about the note?"

"It was stupid, really. Someone stuck it in the pocket of my raincoat the day of Bunny Baldwin's funeral. When I found it, I was furious. I had no intention of being blackmailed and at that point I had no idea you were even pregnant. So I just shoved it in my pocket and forgot about it," he explained.

"If you had known I was pregnant then, would it have made a difference?"

"In my paying blackmail?"

"Yes."

"No. I might have been surprised when I found out you were pregnant, Lily. But I was never ashamed of it and I was never unhappy about it. I knew I wanted the baby and I wanted you."

"Then I'm really not the reason you decided not to run for the senate?"

"Oh, you are the reason. You and our baby. But not because I'm ashamed of you. It's because I want to spend as much time as I can with you and our children."

"Children?" she repeated.

He smiled. "I'm hoping we'll have about half a dozen."

"Not unless you're willing to carry half of them."

He sobered. "If I could and if I thought it would make up for what I caused to happen to you, I would. I would do anything to make up for that. I'm so sorry, Lily."

"It's not your fault, Jack. I'm the one who jumped to conclusions and put myself and our baby in danger. I should have trusted you."

"I want you to," he told her.

And she did trust him, Lily admitted. "Do you have any idea who sent you that blackmail note?"

He shook his head. "I would have said it was Bunny, but she was already dead when the note showed up in my coat pocket."

Mention of Bunny reminded her of Abby and Bunny's missing journals. "Jack, Abby said someone stole her mother's journals. It's possible the person who took them wrote the note. You know how Bunny kept everything in her journals."

"You're right. But who?"

"I don't know. But I think we need to take that note to the police. Abby's already asked them to open a new inquest into the cause of Bunny's death."

"Why?" he asked.

"Because Abby thinks Bunny might have been murdered and whoever stole her journals may be the one responsible for killing her."

"Why would somebody murder Bunny over a bunch of journals?"

"Maybe it was what was in those journals that they murdered her for. If she knew about us and someone tried to blackmail you, there were probably others."

"You're right," he told her. "I'll let Abby know about the letter and that I'm taking it to the police."

The door burst open and in came a flock of Cartwrights. "Oh, thank heavens, you're awake," Sandra declared as she came rushing over to the bed to hug Lily.

"Mother, stop squeezing the stuffing out of Lily. Can't you see she's been in an accident and is in pain?"

"I know very well she's been in an accident, Jack Cartwright. I'm just glad to see the girl is okay." She looked back at Lily and her voice softened. "You *are* okay, aren't you Lily dear?"

"Yes, Sandra. I'm fine. A little banged up, but I'm told I'll be okay."

"You gave us all quite a scare," John Cartwright told her. "Especially my son. I was about ready to ask the doctor to sedate the boy."

Courtney came over to the bed. "When my brother springs you from this place, I'll come over with my make-up kit and see what we can do to cover those nasty bruises and cuts."

"The last thing I think Lily is worried about is her makeup," Elizabeth informed her younger sister. "When you're ready to sue the idiot truck driver who hit you, give me a call. You're family, so I'll waive my fee."

"Since the idiot truck driver she hit works for my trucking company, you'll need to speak with me," Scott Falcon told Elizabeth. Then he turned to her and said, "Lily, next time you want to play tag with a semi, pick someone else's trucking company."

Lily was still laughing when Abby came into the room, followed by Felicity, Emma, Vanessa and Mary. "Hey, I thought we had a sick girl in here," Abby began. "But it sounds to me like you're having a party."

"If we're having a party, I would certainly love some ice cream," Lily announced.

"I'll ask the doctor if you can have some," Elizabeth said.

"Sure she can have it," Courtney declared. "I'm going to find her some. She likes butter pecan."

"You're not going to find butter pecan ice cream in a hospital," Scott said and followed Courtney out.

Sandra came over and kissed Lily's cheek. "Well, I'm going to go make you a big pot of soup for when you get home. I've got this new recipe for tortilla soup that I've been dying to try."

Jack rolled his eyes.

His father grimaced. "I guess I'd better go with her. Maybe I can try to salvage it so that you won't end up back in the hospital after eating it."

"We need to go, too," Abby announced. "We just wanted to be sure you were okay."

After Lily had told them all goodbye, she and Jack were the only ones left.

He came to her bedside again and took her hand. "There's something I meant to give to you at our anniversary dinner, but I never got the chance."

"I don't need any more presents, Jack."

"This one is different." He removed a slip of paper from his pocket and handed it to her.

"What is this?"

"It's the name of a woman who claims to have known your mother."

Lily stared at the folded slip of paper. "But how?"

"I hired a detective to try to pick up the trail where your last investigator left off. He finally came up with a name. He's the man I was meeting last night. That's why I asked you to drive yourself to the restaurant."

"But why? Why did you do this?"

"Because I love you. Because I know it's something you've been searching for your whole life. I thought…I know how much you want to be a part of a family, to find out who your family is or was. I thought…I thought maybe if you had the answers about your past, then you might be able to put it behind you and trust me, love me. I want you to live with me in the present and build a future with me."

Lily stared at the slip of paper that held the answers to her past, the answers she'd searched for her entire life. Then she looked at Jack, the man she loved, the father of her child. She thought about all the people who were in her room tonight, the people who cared about her, worried about her, loved her.

She tore the sheet of paper in half and let it fall to the floor. "I don't need to find my family, Jack. I already have. You are my family and wherever you are is home."

* * * * *

Don't miss the next installment of
SECRET LIVES OF SOCIETY WIVES
Coming in June 2006!
Look for
THE SOON-TO-BE-DISINHERITED WIFE
by
Jennifer Greene
from
Silhouette Desire.

Paying the Playboy's Price

(Silhouette Desire #1732)

by

EMILIE ROSE

Juliana Alden is determined to have her last—
her only—fling before settling down. And she's
found the perfect candidate: bachelor Rex Tanner.
He's pure playboy charm…but can she afford
his price?

Trust Fund Affairs: They've just spent a fortune—
the bachelors had better be worth it.

Don't miss the other titles in this series:

EXPOSING THE EXECUTIVE'S SECRETS (July)
BENDING TO THE BACHELOR'S WILL (August)

On sale this June from Silhouette Desire.

*Available wherever books are sold, including most
bookstores, supermarkets, discount stores and drugstores.*

HOTEL MARCHAND

**Four sisters.
A family legacy.
And someone is out to destroy it.**

A captivating new limited continuity, launching June 2006

The most beautiful hotel in New Orleans,
and someone is out to destroy it. But mystery,
danger and some surprising family revelations
and discoveries won't stop the Marchand sisters
from protecting their birthright…
and finding love along the way.

This riveting new saga begins with

In the Dark

by national bestselling author

JUDITH ARNOLD

The party at Hotel Marchand is in full swing when the lights suddenly go out. What does head of security Mac Jensen do first? He's torn between two jobs—protecting the guests at the hotel and keeping the woman he loves safe.

A woman to protect. A hotel to secure. And no idea who's determined to harm them.

On Sale June 2006

If you enjoyed what you just read,
then we've got an offer you can't resist!

Take 2 bestselling
love stories FREE!

Plus get a FREE surprise gift!

![Silhouette Desire logo]

COMING NEXT MONTH

#1729 HEIRESS BEWARE—Charlene Sands
The Elliotts
She was about to expose her family's darkest secrets, but then she lost her memory and found herself in a stranger's arms.

#1730 SATISFYING LONERGAN'S HONOR—
Maureen Child
Summer of Secrets
Their passion had been denied for far too many years. But will secrets of a long-ago summer come between them once more?

#1731 THE SOON-TO-BE-DISINHERITED WIFE—
Jennifer Greene
Secret Lives of Society Wives
He didn't know if their romantic entanglement was real, or a ruse in order to secure her multimillion-dollar inheritance.

#1732 PAYING THE PLAYBOY'S PRICE—Emilie Rose
Trust Fund Affairs
Desperate to break free of her good-girl image, this society sweetheart bought herself a bachelor at an auction. But what would her stunt really cost her?

#1733 FORCED TO THE ALTAR—Susan Crosby
Rich and Reclusive
Her only refuge was his dark and secretive home. His only salvation was her acceptance of his proposal.

#1734 A CONVENIENT PROPOSITION—Cindy Gerard
Pregnant and alone, she entered into a marriage of convenience… never imagining her attraction to her new husband would prove so *in*convenient.

SDCNM0506